Jane Rawson was born and raised in Canberra and now lives in Melbourne's west with a bagel-baking husband and two good-looking cats. For money, she writes about technology and social justice for a non-profit IT company. Her first novel, *A wrong turn at the Office of Unmade Lists* (Transit Lounge, 2013), was shortlisted for the Aurealis Award for Best Science Fiction Novel and won the Small Press Network's Most Underrated Book Award. Her nonfiction guide to surviving and living with climate change, *The Handbook*, is published by Transit Lounge.

web: janebryonyrawson.wordpress.com
twitter: @frippet

FORMALDEHYDE

JANE RAWSON

First published in Seizure by Xoum in 2015
Xoum Publishing
PO Box Q324, QVB Post Office,
NSW 1230, Australia

www.seizureonline.com
www.xoum.com.au

ISBN 978-1-921134-60-9 (print)
ISBN 978-1-921134-61-6 (digital)

Cataloguing-in-publication data is available from the
National Library of Australia

Internal design and typesetting © Xoum Publishing 2015
Cover design by David Henley

Edited by Marisa Wikramanayake

*Viva La Novella 3 was made possible through the generous support of
Pamela Hewitt and Xoum Publishing*

For Christine Hirst

2022: PAUL

Not knowing I was dead, I went about my business that day like I did on every other. I squashed onto the bus the way I did every morning and everyone else squashed on too. The man next to me rubbed up against my arm a little, told me I looked real smart while I pretended not to hear, while I stared at my phone and wondered whether to ask the new intern on a date.

We pulled up at the corner where the grubby white kids hang out, angling for change. 'Hey, got a dollar, got a dollar, man I need a sandwich, can you help me get a cup of coffee?'; signs on cardboard 'hey why lye I need beer', 'got a spare cigarette, buddy, buddy, got a spare cigarette, got a spare dollar, can you spare a dollar'. All their dogs on strings.

A boy tried to get on the bus. 'Hey man, I got no money, but I gotta get to court by nine. Man, I gotta get to court by nine or they'll arrest me! C'mon man.'

And I thought, well, why didn't you get out of bed earlier, fool – it's not like it's a long walk. The bus driver said, 'Hey, no cash, no ride.' And he tried to shut the door on the kid's hand, shut him out of the bus, but the kid wouldn't move.

'Get outta the way,' the driver yelled at him. 'I got working people gotta get downtown here!'

Yeah, look at these hardworking people, kid, with their daydreams about screwing, and the way they sit all day at their desks staring out the window, sending smartass emails to their jaded friends, drinking too much coffee, working about exactly not at all. Hey scum, these decent people have jobs, you know: you've got no job, you useless little shit, so fuck off.

I looked – not very hard, sure, but I was sort of looking – for my wallet so I could grab him a couple of dollars so he could get on the damn bus, despite his idiocy. But the driver closed the door on him and pulled away from the kerb and most of us went back to fiddling with our phones and our watches. I realised I didn't have any money in my wallet anyway.

If I had money, I'd have bought a cup of coffee before I got on the bus. I made coffee this morning, like I usually do, but I forgot to put the water in the bottom of the percolator. You can wait a long time for coffee to brew when there's no water in the percolator. So that's why I was late this morning. That, and refusing to get out of bed, but that's standard.

So I walked into the office and it was ten to ten, and no one even looked up, and no one yelled at

2

me and I thought, really, this is what's wrong with modern society. No goddamn discipline. How can I be expected to act like a decent human being when no one defines and enforces the boundaries of my behaviour?

I sat down at my desk and turned on my computer and there was absolutely nothing in my calendar. Nothing. Not a single stakeholder briefing, not one mind-mapping workshop, not even a one-on-one coffee catch-up. Every single meeting I'd had booked – all twelve of them for the day – had been cancelled. Something must be going on: there was probably some sort of meeting about it at, like, 9.15 or some ungodly hour, which I'd missed, and everyone was just assuming I was up to speed. I'd have asked one of my pod-mates what the deal was, but they were all in a meeting.

I went to the kitchen to get my reusable takeaway coffee cup, thinking I'd fill in time by heading down-stairs for a macchiato, but it wasn't there. I went into the bathroom to check my hair, spent a little while getting it just right, then looked for my cup again. It definitely wasn't there. So I went back to my desk to see if, well, anything had changed in my absence.

Nope. Everyone was still in a meeting and no one had invited me.

And while I was standing and staring at my monitor, Louise popped her head out from the board room and gestured for me to come over. When I was a foot away she stage whispered in my direction, 'Paul, will you please leave. You're making everyone uncomfortable.'

So I did. Cause I didn't know what else to do.

2000: DEREK

The streetcar stuttered a little and the nurse reached out for something to hang on to. Finding nothing, he swayed and nearly fell.

God, why do they have to pack so many people onto these things, he thought, trying to insert his fingers between the hands clutching the nearest pole. There was a girl dressed as some kind of rabbit in bondage with her hand below his, a Chinese guy with his hand above, and a skinny little man clinging to some sort of deformed Maltese terrier holding the pole above him.

It was lucky the ride was smooth enough for each of them to hold on with only one hand, as every last one of them had their other hand full of Dostoevsky's *The Idiot*. He'd never read it himself; he'd read *Crime & Punishment* years ago, but apart from Raskolnikov falling down and vomiting a lot, nothing much of it stuck with him.

The Dostoevsky, the jolting back and forth, the park full of cats, the methanol seeping out of that bloke's pores: I bloody hate the commute, he thought. Dostoevsky? What the hell is wrong with you people? Get yourself a damn copy of *Men are from Mars; Women are from Venus* or *Java script for those one step away from vegetative* will you and stop pretending you're enjoying that anachronistic codswallop. You're not impressing anyone, you know.

So when the streetcar slammed hard into something and the people were screaming and there was the falling and more of the screaming and copies of *The Idiot* were drifting in a pretentious snow around him, he was kind of relieved. What with everyone falling to the floor and the tumbling out the gaping hole where the front of the car used to be, he seemed to be the only one left holding on to the pole. He took a second to savour his victory. The Chinese guy was nowhere to be seen. He looked out at the park and saw that the deformed dog had escaped and was chasing cats, while rabbit girl had come to rest in a furry, flopsy lump on the floor. The nurse – Derek – reached down to give the bunny a hand to get to her feet, but the hand pulled right away from her little bunny sleeve in a gush of blood. Despite both his medical training and his loathing of the stereotypes of 19th century Russian literature, he followed a brief spate of vomiting with some serious falling down.

When the ambulance came, she was curled up on his recovered lap. He was reading aloud from the pages strewn about, over her snuffly snores, over the wail of sirens:

Towards the end of November, during a thaw, at nine o'clock one morning, a train on the Warsaw and Petersburg railway was approaching the latter city at full speed . . . Some of the passengers by this particular train were returning from abroad; but the third-class carriages were the best filled, chiefly with insignificant persons of various occupations and degrees, picked up at the different . . .

He picked up another page.

'Be quiet, Ivan Fedorovitch! Leave me alone' cried Mrs Epanchin. 'Why do you offer me your arm now? You had not sense enough to take me away before . . .'

And as they lifted her onto a gurney, he retrieved an un-torn, only slightly bloodied copy of *The Idiot* from under a broken body and stuffed it in his bag.

2000: AMY

Plucking the quail off the bones, sucking the smell of you off my fingers. Slumped here alone in your ridiculous under-used hot tub, drinking champagne, feeling the bubbles through my veins, on my skin – my head hurts. It's hot in here.

My gut hurts from wanting you. Triangles on my cheeks are numb. Thinking about you I feel myself get hot, but like it's someone else feeling it. Like intravenous valium. I think about biting down on the softness of your top lip, that first time, like I had a right to be so rash with your perfect skin. Drunk then, like now, forgetting protocol. I'd imagined it so many times I just flat-out forgot to be polite.

The smell of you now just the same as it was then. And you, even prettier – heartbreakingly implausibly fucking beautiful – even prettier close up than you were on the airbrushed posters hung above the bed of every horny teenage boy in the country.

From that very first time, I couldn't imagine even thinking about caring about Derek. I'd loved him, my husband: I had. But there just wasn't space in my brain any more: each living breath was all about you, every neuron firing just for the thinking of you. Who would have thought it possible that a full-grown human being could actually, in real life, have both their last clear thought of the day and their very first thought on waking be about exactly the same thing: you. But there you have it.

Licking the taste of you off my fingers, the taste of you off my lips. Dreaming the smell of you.

Last night in my dream we were lying in your bed, your naked torso lined with the scars of a babyhood in hospitals. Scars winding spirals around your belly; a spiral staircase and I'm walking down into your navel. I asked you if your mother was scared those days, when you were a tiny scrap of flesh in a plastic box, all tubes and wires; if her brain fuzzed with the white noise of terror every minute you breathed like a machine; if you'd ever bothered to ask her. But when you answered your voice was a giant hum in the cavern of your belly and I didn't know the language.

Listening to you now on the stereo I'm a little more awake than then, but grasping even less of what you're saying to me.

So are you coming home tonight?

—

The door.

'Hey honey, I'm home.'

The sound of you in the suite's kitchen, glass on glass and the tumbling ice from your frost-free fridge.

'I'm in here.' I want you here right now. 'Come to bed.'

'Yup, just a sec. Just grabbing a drink.'

And here's you, you in the doorframe, you all dressed in black. Satiny black shirt with the buttons just one hole off, but who cares, I can see the curve of your gorgeous breast where the shirt doesn't quite close right. Look at your fucking glorious curves and the curls of your hair, your much-dreamed-about belly button peeking out above the waistband of your suede hipsters. Look how smooth your brown stomach is; just look for a second, will you? This would be easier if you could be just a tiny bit less perfect.

You sit on the edge of the bed and set your drink down.

'How are you my handsome woman?' You slide your little hand under the sheets and give my nipple a squeeze.

'Ouch. Be a bit careful, would you?'

'Who's a grumpy squirrel?' You retrieve your hand and use it instead to have a drink. 'What's up, baby?'

'I just missed you.'

'A gal's gotta work, honey, you know that.'

'Well, when did your show finish?' I try to keep the

whine out of my voice, but it's there, it's there. You're trying to turn alternative but your record company has wrung a last few stadium sets out of you and we both know the teen fans who fill stadiums have to be home at a reasonable hour.

'Stop trying to see what time it is.' You have another drink. 'My show finished at eleven, which you know perfectly well, and it's now 2 am which means I've been out without you for four hours.' You give me your best paparazzi smile. 'You could've come you know.'

'I'm an embarrassment.'

'What? Who said that?' You push my fringe out of my face and run your thumb across the skin beside my eye.

'Are you trying to uncrease my wrinkles?' I try to sound like I'm joking but it's obvious that I'm not.

'Oh, Amy. What is it now? Is it Dion again?'

'It isn't Dion. I can't come to your shows, I'm too old. You can't be seen with me. What about your fans?' We both know it's my genitals that are the issue, not my age.

'I can't be seen with my hand up your skirt, but that doesn't mean I can't be seen with you.' And you run your hand up my thigh, my belly, between my legs. 'I want to be seen with you,' you whisper, your other hand ringing my ankle, fingers trapping my butterfly tattoo.

I don't understand why I feel so angry with you.

'I'm getting another drink,' you say, draining the last third of the one in your hand. 'Shall I get one for you?'

I shake my head, but then I regret it and follow you into the kitchen.

'I just wish you'd come home sooner,' I say before I've even thought about why. 'What do you see in those guys? Why are you even out with those guys?' I'm keeping my voice low, even. This time maybe we can just talk about it and you'll see what I mean and instead of going out every night you'll come home and curl up beside me and I'll read you a bedtime story and we'll fall asleep in each other's arms.

'Dion? Nam? Because they're my friends, Amy.' You knock back another drink. 'They're my friends and they're not too uptight to come out with me and have a good time. I can't come home after the show and go to bed, Jesus, Amy! I have people I have to spend time with and anyway, I'm too wired. Why can't you get it?'

Friends? They're your accessories. You want to show people your Christian country-pop past is behind you. You want everyone talking about which one of these gorgeous guys you're with – is it the guitarist from that emo-metal band? Is it the star of last year's art-house sensation? Is it both of them? At once?

'Fucking Dion, you know he tried to grope me last time he was here,' I mutter and I don't know if that's even true, maybe it was me groping him. It's all pretty blurry now. It was all pretty blurry then.

'That's not how I remember it,' you say, and you're pouring another.

'Slow down!' I tell you. 'We have to be in the studio by 10.'

'Fuck, Amy, can you just go back on the pill? I can't handle your moods any more!'

'It's not my fucking moods, *Faith*!' I yell at you. 'It's your fucking friends and you never wanting to be seen with me. You're ashamed of me!'

'Well I am right now,' you say, and you take your drink and walk out the door.

I want to go home. No, not that home. The home I have with you, the home I'm homesick for – the future imaginary home. I want to be sitting there, in a big, green armchair, the arms worn down. The chair sits in a rectangle of sunshine; the owner of the house (who is, perhaps, me) has slid the window open to let the warm breeze blow in. I'm sitting in the chair, sitting in the sunshine. My hair is in braids. I'm wearing a gingham dress. It's a frock really; a gingham frock. It's stretched over my tummy, which is distended because I'm pregnant. There's a baby inside me, and I'm sitting in the sunshine, on my chair, looking out the window at the rows of grain, not in our yard where we'd have to look after them, but next door, where they're not our problem but they are our view.

Our garden is green and has apple trees. There's a cat sleeping under one of them. Sometimes there are miniature cows, three foot tall at the shoulder, caramel-brown, but today they're somewhere else.

And there's you, curled on the floor at my feet, with your head resting on my belly and your hand on my knee, and you're almost asleep. I'm stroking your beautiful hair, and you love me. You love me.

I can't have this argument again. Today I can't cry to break your heart, cry to make you quiet, cry to make it stop. Today I don't want to wait for you to go to sleep, wake up tomorrow and tell me sorry (and know that what you mean is, 'Please don't quit. I need you behind the desk miraculously transforming me from angelic songbird to underground poet').

So today, tonight, I go to your bedroom and put on my clothes, I put on my shoes while you take the elevator down to the street, stomp around to the corner where you'll smoke a cigarette and turn around and come right back because you've thought of something else you need to tell me, because you want to remind me yet again that no one calls you Faith any more, it's Audrey, and can I please get with the program. But by the time you're back I'll have my bag and I'll walk out the door past you and I won't listen to what you're saying and I'll ignore the feeling, the one that goes, 'God, I love you so much, god, I'm so sorry, I love you, I love you, I love you, please hold me, please love me again, please love me' and I'll walk out the door and hail a cab and get in it and I'll go away and I won't come back.

Only it doesn't quite happen like that. This time you walk around the corner to smoke, and you don't come back. And this time I can't find my keys. And without the keys I can't lock the door behind me, and if I leave the door open someone will steal your guitars and they're worth about a hundred thousand dollars and if someone stole them you'd be broken-hearted (much more so than you'll be to lose me).

It won't take you more than a week to get over me, no more than a month to forget I was ever here: god, you were always going to be gone as soon as we wrapped this album. Your friends don't like me, your fans don't even know I exist. But we had something: I don't know what it was, but it was something. I can't let you just forget.

So I shut myself in the bathroom with a sizeable kitchen knife and my notebook and one of my two pens, and I write you a note. Then I call an ambulance and hack my arm off below the elbow, taking care to tie-off first – I don't want to die or anything overly dramatic. And the ambulance takes me away and takes care of the whole problem with the front door, which is exactly what you'd hope for from the emergency services.

—

A note:

I'm leaving my arm here to remind you.
Remember how this was?

The way your feet moved. The bits of hair that
stood up, the ones that lay flat. Your incisors like
a dog's when you grinned, your eyes wide and
surprised at joy. The softness in the palm of your
hand.

I'm leaving my arm here for you. Suspend it in
formaldehyde; suspend it in alcohol.

Hold my hand. You're safe here – hold my hand.

—

Watching him sleep now, back here in our bed again.
How did I end up back here again? My tummy
swelling under my department store pyjamas (no
gingham frocks, no armchairs, but never mind). My
belly full of dreams of spiral staircases, of hospital
scars.

Derek didn't ask. Didn't ask where I'd been all those
months, about my belly or about the arm. He had
started stretching diagonally across the bed though,
I noticed.

Where did you come from, little child? How did
you get from there to here? I've heard stories about hot
tubs but never believed them. And some would talk
about the unstoppable power of love, but really, it was

never love, was it? I don't know what it was but it had none of the kindness of love. Love wasn't the vector for the scrap of skin growing inside me.

I hope it wasn't pain; hope it wasn't tears. I hope it was the armchair and the cat in the fruit trees.

2022: PAUL

I had probably slid sideways out of society, being unemployed, but it didn't feel like it. The guy outside McDonald's still tried to hold the door open for me, cup thrust out, as I passed by. The driver glanced at my bus pass just like he had every day before. People avoided sitting next to me. I still couldn't find which page of *The Idiot* I was up to.

I felt a little lazy, having not yelled or demanded an explanation or bought a gun and gone back and picked off my former co-workers, but really the situation was ideal. What could be better than not having to go to work? Ever again?

I got off the bus at the park. Not much reason to do or not do anything but looking out the window at the park I saw the people out walking their cats and it seemed like a good place to be. The sunshine, all those people who don't seem to have any reason to go to work either, all setting a good example for someone who's new to the fold, all still clean and smiling. And there were the cats. Reason enough.

I lay down on the grass on my back. The sun was on my face. I closed my eyes and looked at the red of my eyelids and the black hole where the sun used to be, and thought about nothing. Someone was licking my fingertips. A head inserted itself between my hand and the grass. A back rubbed against the sole of my foot. And they climbed on top of me, the cats: paws kneading my stomach, a claw in my nipple. Cats curling up over my throat, a tail flicking across my mouth, purring hard up against my cheekbone. And I felt cats flopping fat bodies on my tender groin, cat stomachs against my face, kittens with their tongues in my ears, and I drifted off and enjoyed my new life.

—

'Yep. Yep. Yeah . . . Dad, I said yes. I know. Yes, I know. No. No, of course not. Dad! Look, I'm going to. I have every intention. No, I don't need you to. Really. NO, REALLY. It'll be fine. It's OK. No, I sent the form in days ago. I don't know; they said maybe six weeks. What's the point if they said six weeks? It's only been a few days. No, it's OK. I'm fine, really. OK. OK, thanks Dad. Yep. Yep. Yeah, I will. Alright. Talk to you soon.'

So now I had to go to the Identity Office, because apparently I went last week.

They checked me for guns on my way in and I took

a number and a seat, closed my eyes, and listened in on the conversation as it slipped in and out of *Divorce Court*.

'Don't touch my stuff.'

'I'm not touching your stuff.'

'Yes you were. You had your leg next to my bag.'

'Next to isn't touching.'

'Close enough.'

'Oh for fuck's sake.'

'What did you say?'

'I said, "Oh for fuck's sake".'

'Don't you swear at me!'

'I wasn't swearing *at* you.'

'Yes you were.'

'I was swearing at the world in general.'

'Don't get smart. Don't get smart with me!'

'Oh for Christ's sake!'

'Don't swear at me!'

And so on. When I checked back in one of them was calling security because the other one was threatening to go home and get her gun.

The loudspeaker crackled: 'Number 65.'

That's me.

I had to duck to talk into the microphone set into the plexiglass. Bending over distorted my 'I just want this to go smoothly for both of us' smile. I worried that I looked crazy, or frightening. Worried that I looked like I was one of them.

'Hi. How are you?'

'How can we help you?'

'I'd like to apply for unemployment assistance.'

'Take this form and a number. Fill in the form and come back to the desk when your number is called.'

'Oh. Do you have a pen?'

'We don't provide pens.'

'I see.'

This wasn't going very well so far.

I went back to my seat, only it wasn't my seat any more. Some hugely, morbidly fat guy had taken possession of it, and after all, why not? It's not like I own the place.

A tiny girl with a nose like an elf's was fixing her creamy, shiny blue eyeshadow, staring intently into a Hello Kitty pocket mirror. She was all urban-realist pockets, hooded sweatshirt, seriously rubbery, nubbly runners, and in the V of her slightly unzipped décolletage, what looked like the top of a whispery dorsal fin, the hint of a yakuza-style vibrant orange koi.

'Excuse me,' I said.

She was wearing headphones. And she was probably carrying a very tiny, very feminine, probably Hello Kitty-ornamented, knife somewhere on her person, so I was a little leery of tapping her bare (knee-socks, but of course) knee.

I waved my hand in front of her face. She looked at me, but didn't remove her headphones.

'Excuse me.'

She was still gazing blankly at me so I soldiered on.

'Do you have a pen I could borrow?'

She pushed back her furry, ear-adorned hat and pulled out her earbuds.

'Sorry?'

'Do you have a pen I could borrow?'

'Oh, shuuuure. One sec.'

The pen she handed me was not, as I had assumed it would be, dangling tiny star twins or encrusted with sparkles. It was a chewed 2B pencil, regulation school-issue yellow.

'Thanks.' There was a slightly awkward pause as I weighed up issues of propriety versus the demands of bureaucracy. 'Not to be, you know, ungrateful or anything, but you don't have an actual pen, do you?'

'Sorry. I'm allergic to ink.'

'Oh. I'm sorry to hear that.'

She had a very cute smile which I guess was for the best. Appropriate and all.

'Never mind then. I'll see what I can do with this. Can you spare it for five minutes or so?'

'Oh, shuuuure.'

I got to work.

Name: Paul Crawford.

Easy.

Identity Number: I wrote it down.

Address: yep. Phone Number: yep.

Last Job: Database administrator.

Reason for Leaving Last Job: they asked me to.

Bank account, outstanding debts, car registration (don't have one), licence number (nope, not one of those) et cetera, et cetera.

Sign here. So I did.

'Thanks.' Holding out the pencil.

She left both hat and headphones on this time, looked up from reading my form, and extended her hand palm up. I placed the pencil in it gently, and she refused to break eye contact. I'd never seen someone blink so languorously before. This blink, in fact, was what the word languor was invented for.

She readjusted her ears and her head bounced back and forth and she looked at her watch, propped her feet up on the chair in front and closed her eyes.

Fine.

I sat and sat and sat and sat and watched the clock hands go round and entertained myself with extremely detailed lascivious ponderings, with special reference to how tight the elastic on her doubtless anime-adorned underpants legs was. Just how many fingers could I slide under there?

I was so absorbed in this thought that I didn't notice she had got up until I saw the brown-yellow door of the bathroom swinging shut behind her. It smelled bad in there. I was surprised when she didn't look back over her shoulder in an inviting fashion:

wasn't that how these things were supposed to go?

One of the digital slivers was missing from the flashing 'your number's up' indicator. Eight wasn't quite; four was almost incomprehensible. And they were counting through the almost-eighties but not quite, up to 82 now. I was 86. I could barely wait.

'Keyshawn, you take that thing outta your mouth Right Now.'

'Police sources described the head as thus far absent. When asked why dogs are not being used in the search, a police spokesman pointed out that dogs were what had got them in this position in the first place.'

83. 84.

'But how can that be? I was in the house when you called. I *know* I was in the house when you called because this is the first time I've left the house this year. No, *really*. I can't believe you dragged me down here for this.'

85.

'And so I told him, yeah, the gun was mine but, hell, weren't me that used it. And he was all like, well, if it weren't you, who the hell was it? Well, shit, y'know, I don't *know* who it was. If I *knew*, don't cha think I'd be kicking their ass right now? Huh? Damn, whoever that was has got me in one mess of trouble.'

86.

I stood up slowly. Had a little stretch. Hoped she'd

come back. She didn't. Followed the flashing lights and dipped my head to the window-set microphone.

'Hi.'

'Hello. How can we help you today?'

'I've got this unemployment form to file.'

'Pass it through the drawer, please.'

I did.

'This form is filled in in pencil.'

'I know.'

'It needs to be filled in in pen.'

'I'm sorry.'

'Take another form, please, and fill it in in pen. You'll need to take a new number too.'

'But I don't have a pen.'

'Next.'

The girl with the pencil was gone. So I left too.

2000: BENJAMIN

She woke up from the anaesthetic with a start, gripped by a dream of balancing tip-toes above shark-filled waters. The tubes in her nostrils tugged and tore, the dry scraping pulled her head back to the pillow.

Dark.

Tears slipped down her face and she sobbed, once, though she felt nothing much. Nothing much in her arm, less in her head. Just the silvery residue of nightmare tears.

Where was everyone?

Moonlight – streetlight? – brightened the thin nylon curtain and blushed her eyelids as she tried to go back to sleep. She was uncomfortable. The light was bright, her nose hurt, her tongue stuck to the roof of her mouth, she was awake but so asleep, she was dreaming awake of drinking water, her arm was beginning to ache and she could taste acid bile in the cavities of her teeth. Had she been vomiting?

She wanted to piss. She wanted to drink and she

wanted to piss, and she was stuck here, bound up through her nostrils and her veins, and she couldn't move and she didn't know the protocol for getting someone to save her. Could someone please come here and save me from this?

'Hello?'

It was a pathetic inflection. No one heard, of course.

She cleared her throat and tried again.

'Excuse me?'

'Yes?'

Um, no, hang on, what? That wasn't what she'd intended.

'Um, oh . . .'

'Pardon?'

'Sorry.'

'Didn't you say "excuse me?"?'

'The nurse. Sorry. I was calling the nurse.'

'Oh. Right. Sorry.'

She didn't want to say excuse me again. She hadn't thought there would be someone right there. She felt stupid saying excuse me again. But god, she wanted someone to come and release her from all of this.

She chewed on her lip and tried not to think about it, but did.

'You should call louder.'

'Oh it wasn't anything. It doesn't matter.'

'Are you sure? Maybe I can . . .'

'It's nothing. Sorry.'

'Righto.'

They slept. He slept and she, somehow reabsorbing urine into her bloodstream, and despite the streetlight still stark upon her face, slept too.

When she woke up it was foggy, like a sodden poodle pressed against the window, and she felt like she'd been having other people's dreams. The nurse was over her, not looking at her, tugging at the needle and slowly extracting tubing from under the skin of her arm.

'Sheew. Ah!'

'Oh, hello. You're awake.'

'M.'

'Does this hurt?'

'No. It's fine.'

'Won't be a minute. I'll just tape this up and . . . there. All alright now?'

New tubing to new needle, new white bandage wrapped over the whole. The hole.

'Now let's have a look at that other arm.'

New arm.

The bandage, from fingertips to throat, was mapped with brown, sticky stains. Seepage. She felt impolite, seeping like that in this clean white place. Embarrassed.

'That'll need new bandages. How does it feel?'

'It hurts a bit.'

'Can you show me where?'

She didn't want to move her other hand. When she moved, she could feel the tubing tug inside her vein. She tried to point without moving, moved anyway, and felt her stomach heave.

'Oh. Um, I think I'm going to . . . oh–'

Blood and bile spilled over her chin and her involuntarily raised hand and splashed the strange purple-green pattern already splashed across the nurse's front.

'Oh god, I'm sorry. I – '

And again . . .

One embarrassment after another. Her life had become some sort of calculated logic of humiliation. Who was planning this stuff?

It had started with the job promoting Bound – basically a dungeon masquerading as a dinner-theatre, with a sideline in catering for and entertaining at children's parties – which mostly involved standing outside the door of the 'theatre' in a flesh-coloured body stocking, keeping warm by means of the dog collar and studded wrist-cuffs which supplemented it, and handing out fliers on the night's show. Then, a few weeks back, the misguided management had decided the theatre should embrace the Christian spirit and put on an Easter show. While the rabbit suit (dog collar and cuffs to be worn over, not under, the acrylic fur) certainly did a little more to keep out the wind, it was no less embarrassing than the body stocking. At least she *looked* hot in the body stocking.

And then – the accident. It wasn't enough that she had to deal with the pain and the blood and the fear and the whole spontaneous amputation business, she had had to deal with all of that while wearing a rabbit suit. The guy who'd helped her had been entirely lovely about the rabbit suit; in fact, he'd barely mentioned it, apart from calling her Benjamin Bunny on one occasion. He'd bundled her up in blazers and cardigans no longer needed by her various dead former fellow passengers, and stopped the bleeding with a seatbelt torn from the wheelchair restraint. Throughout the experience, he'd worn his blue elasticized nurse hat, the professionalism of which had lulled her pounding, terrified little heart into a state of trusting repose until she'd fallen asleep in his long-legged lap.

And in her dreams:

Why do you offer me your arm now?

2022: PAUL

When I got home that day – the day I didn't get unemployment benefits – I discovered I no longer had one. Yellow police CAUTION tape was strung across my front steps. I ducked under it to read the notice taped to my front door.

'This dwelling is currently under investigation by the police. Do not enter. All enquiries should be directed to the Precinct 9 police station.'

Obviously, this was a little inconvenient. My stuff, for starters, was in there, including the bathroom, which I really needed to use. I would have quite liked to get a coat, as the sun was going down and a stiff breeze had picked up. I sat in the doorway and considered my options. Passers-by didn't give me a second glance.

Option 1: disregard police notice, go into house, go to the toilet, drink beer, watch TV, order Indian food, get fatter and older, fall asleep on the couch while thinking about having sex with the pencil girl.

Problems: scared of the law. Plus, my landlord was

just itching for an excuse to kick me out. Also, who knew what the hell was in there? Someone could have used someone else's bleeding neck stump to draw pictures of me with that little toy dog I broke in that store when I was six and never told anyone, not even my dad. Did I really want to deal with that?

Option 2: call my dad, ask him to drive for two hours and come pick me up and take me home. Where home was, you know, the tiny apartment my dad lives in, alone, down the coast, his golden retriever asleep and farting in front of the heater.

Problems: oh, Dad. He's so sweet, but, hell, he would ask questions. Lots of questions. And I didn't feel like it.

Option 3: open door, try not to look around too much (especially don't look into the lounge room or kitchen, cause that's where writing with bleeding stumps always seems to take place) or touch anything, pee, fix my hair, grab my coat and my book, which I was really enjoying and was angry about leaving behind this morning, sneak out, lock door, wipe doorknob with tail of shirt and head for a bar. Worry about everything else later.

All went to plan except I was worried from second one. And when I stepped outside and she was standing at the bottom of the stairs, I almost jumped out of my skin.

'You looked like you were about to jump out of your

skin,' she said. 'Which I suppose wouldn't have been the end of the world. Plenty of prosthetic skins out there that we could have fixed you up with.'

'Are you going to turn me in to the police?' I asked.

'I'm sorry,' she said, 'I don't have my magic wand with me right now.'

'What? Oh, right. Ha.'

'Why, are you breaking the law or something? Isn't this your house? This is the address you wrote with my pencil, isn't it?'

'Yeah, it's my house. But apparently I'm not supposed to go in it.'

'Did you get kicked out?'

'What? Oh, no. Well, sort of. I don't know. Want a beer?'

'I don't drink beer. I would like whiskey.'

'They have whiskey at the place I'm going to.'

'Where are you going to?'

'I don't know. Some place where they have whiskey. Wanna come?'

'OK.'

I asked her if she had a car.

'No,' she said. 'I can't drive.'

'Me neither.'

'I know.'

'Oh, yeah. Um. Well, shall we? You already know my name's Paul, but we have to start somewhere. I'm Paul.'

'I'm Benjamin.'

I frowned at her and waited for her to take it back. She didn't.

'Oh, you are not. Don't fib.'

'Am too,' she said.

'Really?'

'Yup. Am now, anyway.'

'Fair enough. Nice to meet you, Benjamin. Thanks for the pencil.'

'My pleasure.'

And she smiled again like she had that afternoon, and I got a little tingle right in the middle of my lower lip and another one somewhere way down in my guts. We walked. We talked nonsense. Pleasantries. She was really very, very cute. Very cute. We sat. We drank. We drank more. We didn't eat, and yet we kept drinking. Some would call it foolish, but it felt like fun. She drank her whiskey with a splash of water and I wondered why she was drinking like an old man when she looked like a baby bunny. I drank beer till I felt like someone had stuck a bike pump up my ass and blown my intestines drum-tight, then I ordered a scotch and soda: cheap booze. And another, and a couple more.

I spent, I swear, 35 minutes working up the nerve to ask her home, before realising I didn't have a home to ask her to. And then I started wondering where the hell I was going to sleep. It looked cold outside.

I could stay at one of the rooms upstairs, I thought, if my credit card still worked.

But it didn't. They ran it, and the system rejected it, and they ran it again. And it was rejected. I was too drunk to work out why.

'More booze,' I declared.

'Let's go home.' She sounded a lot less drunk than she should have.

'Don't have a home.'

'My home. We can go to my home, that's fine.'

'Really?'

'Oh, you knew I was going to invite you home. Stop it.'

'Orright then.'

'Shall we grab a cab? I think I've had enough to drink.'

'Orright then.'

All a bit blurry. I left my wallet on the bar and had to go back inside and grab it. Man on the TV was still talking about missing heads and I wondered for a second about my living room wall but then I forgot, cause I started thinking about knees instead. Walked out to where it was, indeed, cold.

She was holding the door of a cab open for me. I kissed her warm mouth as I ducked by her to get in. The driver was listening to AC/DC – not the new album, but something from around 1980 – and I laughed.

'I assume you're laughing because you think this is prophetic,' she said a little sternly.

'I couldn't shake a fucking maraca all night long, the amount I've drunk. Just laughing.'

'Aha.' And she chuckled.

'But I could try, if you like.'

'We'll see.' She was still smiling.

She held my hand while I fell a little bit asleep. And when I woke up we were there.

'C'mon chum, outta the car.'

Opening the front door and making the long hike up two flights of narrow stairs.

'Let me give you some money, sweet Benjamin.'

'All taken care of.'

'Thanks.'

'Don't mention it.'

'Too late.'

'Yes. Shut up and come in before the cat gets out.'

She locked the door behind us and turned on the floor lamp.

'Your place is nice.' It was.

'Thanks,' she said. 'I'm going to get myself a drink of water. I could even get one for you too, if you like.'

I nodded and slumped on the sofa.

'Now look,' she said when she reappeared, 'I guess I should clear some things up. I mean, I don't want you to think–'

'Hey, I'm happy to have somewhere to sleep. I'm not pushing my luck.'

'What I meant was, I don't want you to think this is just about giving you somewhere to sleep. I meant, oh–'

She leaned over and kissed me and I realised that I had to sober up fast. I didn't want to miss this. She lifted her hand to touch my face and let it drop back down. So I leaned over and took her hand and kissed her mouth. 'Don't give her time to change her mind,' I thought.

When she kissed me I could feel her fingers grasping mine. She was holding tight enough to hurt. Her kisses were the softest, least-invasive drunk kisses I think I've ever felt, her tongue on my lips but – god! – so infuriatingly, tantalisingly soft, like you might not ever know it had been there, might doubt your memory of it. Everything desperate in her was happening in her kneading, needful hands. Her kneading hand, really; one hand sat quiet in her lap. And when I reached for it, even mid-kiss, she moved it surreptitiously aside, as if by coincidence.

Then she had her hand on my chest, over my breastbone, her face up close to mine; breathing parts of the same air, we were, taking a couple of elements each.

'Will you take your shirt off?' she asked.

I undid the buttons and she slipped it from my shoulders. I could hear her breath, slightly sharp, as her hands moved over the skin of my shoulders.

'Oh, look at the ridge here, a little mountain range

of bone . . .' and all her focus was in her fingers. After a moment I saw her eyes refocus, watched her pulling back from her fingers to find my face again with hers. A guilty look in her smile, like she'd momentarily abandoned me for the landscape of my skin.

No buttons on her shirt, tiny little stretchy thing that it was, emblazoned with some obscure band from the 1980s. She could tug it over her head without any help from me. And it turns out it's not a koi at all, but some sort of weird prehistoric-looking lizard tattooed across her with entirely unlizardish eyes. I reached for her bra.

'Wait a second.'

She unzipped her knee-high boots, leaving on her knee-high black stockings, stood up and squirmed out of her stretchy plaid skirt.

'OK, look. Sit still and look for a second. See how my bra and my undies match each other? See the way my bra makes my cleavage just, well, unbearably alluring? These undies are pretty damn cute, aren't they?' She sat back down. 'OK, go ahead.'

'You look nice.'

'Sorry. It's just, you know, when I was here earlier tonight thinking I might come by your house and see what you were up to and wondering if anything might come of it, I put these on – y'know, just in case. So it'd be a pity if you didn't notice them.'

'When we were in the Identity Office I was thinking about your knickers.'

'Oh, they were different ones.'

'It doesn't really matter. These are yours too. Come here.'

She lay half back on the couch. Leaning over her, I ran my fingers up over her thighs and noted that my whole hand would slide under the elastic of her underpants. Distracted from kissing her face, thumbs hooked over her hips, I adored the line of her bra, licked the skin that dipped along its edges, ran my tongue over the front clasp, chewed at it, worried it, gave in and opened it with my fingers.

'Mmm.' She smiled. 'Thanks. You don't have to keep noticing my underwear now. Your work here is done.'

Oh, it's hard to be glib when your eyes are glazing over from lust. And so, so focused on the way I'm so not getting hard, despite the feeling that every nerve ending my body has ever owned has moved into my groin. Oh god, I'm drunk.

'I'm drunk,' I told her.

'I know. Me too.'

'Um, yeah. But it's kind of different for me.'

'Can you please shut up and bite me there?'

'I . . . oh, OK.'

'Oh, that's exactly right. Oh . . . mmm . . . Get here . . . oh!' A little shriek. A big shriek from me. Ouch! Jesus! Not all my nerve endings are in my groin, apparently.

'Sorry. Sorry. Oops.'

Dislodging her knee from my stomach, where it had shot during the last exchange.

Her eyes are glinting furiously. Her nose wrinkling, her smile like a polar bear cub tearing chunks from its first Eskimo. She flips me over on my back and buries her teeth in my thigh.

'Ow!'

'Ow? Good ow, though, right?'

'Good ow, yes. But ow!'

Her hands under my shoulder blades, she's licking my nipples like they're a cure for something, holding tight as if she might fall off. I can't blame her: I feel like I might fall off too.

'Oh, Benjamin.' Yep, that sounds weird. 'Hey, um, look. I, well, let's be honest. I've been in this situation before and, believe me, it's not going to work.'

'When you say "it" you're not talking about our great love for one another, are you?'

'Um, no. Kinda something a bit more, y'know . . .'

'I don't care. There's plenty of other stuff we can do.'

I so want to. But on the other hand, I so want to go to sleep.

'You want to go to sleep, don't you?' she said.

'No. You're fucking gorgeous. I want to nail you.'

'Ha! God, you're suave. Hey look, asshole, you know you can just go to sleep tonight. And, well, we can wake up all stinky and sweaty and sober enough to notice just how goddamn ugly each of us is and how bad each other's breath smells, and we'll have phenomenal headaches and our guts will be cramping from alcohol poisoning and, well, perhaps we'll feel more like fucking then. Whaddya say?'

'Oh, that sounds like a dream come true.'

'Get your trousers off and get into bed, then.'

Oh, bless her.

I'm sure I snored all night. I'm sure I was obnoxious to be around. But I didn't know a thing about it, because I was pretty much in a coma. I remember dreaming, confusingly real dreams about trying to make it to the bus on time, but none of my dreams were disturbing enough to shake me awake.

When I did wake up, she wasn't in bed any more. So I pulled on my wrinkly, stinky trousers and my tank top, and went in search. She was sitting at the kitchen table, all showered and dressed, jeans and a Jets T-shirt, damp hair curling around her neck, book in hand, coffee cup in front of her.

'Hey, what happened to hot animal sex, young lady?'

'Good morning. Are you saying you don't remember?'

'Don't remember what?'

'The hot animal sex. Baby, you were unbelievable. Grrr! Hard as a rock. And your tongue! Oh my, your tongue!'

'Ah, shut up.'

'Oh, sorry. But you snored so loud I had to get up. Besides, some of us have jobs to go to.'

I looked around. 'Do you actually *have* a cat?'

'Oh, no. I'd like one though. Do you have a spare?'

I went to the bathroom, washed my face, took a piss and wished I'd thought to grab my toothbrush. I put some toothpaste on my fingertip and rubbed it around my mouth. It was pretty unsatisfying.

'Coffee?' From the kitchen.

'Yesh pleash.' I spat and wiped my face. 'Did you say you have to go to work?'

'Uh huh.'

'Um, if you have a job,' I walked back into the kitchen, 'what were you doing at Identity?'

'Hanging out.' She smiled up at me from her book. 'I go there to pick up hot guys.'

For a second I wondered if she was telling the truth. She wasn't telling the truth.

'Disability. I had to go sort out some stuff with my disability pension.'

'Oh.' Trying to come up with something smart to say, everything sounding, shall we say, inappropriate.

'Are you feeling awkward?'

'Little bit.'

'See here,' she put the book down, twisted her arm around and ran her fingers down a scar I'd entirely failed to notice. It ran right the way around her forearm, just below the elbow, the skin above the scar paler than that below. 'My hand doesn't work all that well. I had an accident. It was a long time ago, though.'

'Oh, I'm sorry.'

'It's no big deal. I'm glad I've got an arm at all, really.'

The coffee had dripped. I drank it with good grace.

'So, what are we going to do with you today?' she asked.

'Well, I guess I should try to work out what's going on with my house, and my credit card, and my unemployment money . . . Mostly I'd like to go lie in the park in the sun. Um, hey: thanks so much for the place to stay last night.'

'Tell you what,' she said. 'If you can't get back into your house today, it'd be fine for you to stay here for a while: just a while though, OK? Give me a call at work and let me know what's going on.' She searched among the papers on the table for a blank scrap and a chewed pencil, and wrote down her number. 'Here you go.'

'Oh, you don't have to do that.'

'I know that. If you don't want to stay, you can just say that.'

'Hell, no. I'd love to stay. I'm just being polite. You know, like my dad brought me up to be.'

'Good for your dad. Want to borrow a T-shirt?'

'Um, you're a bit smaller than me.'

'I've got big ones. I sleep in them. When I'm not sleeping naked with saucy guys I pick up off the street, of course.'

'Of course. Well then, sure.'

'Panthers or Titans?'

'You have weird T-shirts.'

'And?'

'Panthers, thanks.'

'And go take a shower, will you? You stink. There's towels in that cupboard. I'll leave a key on the table for you.'

'Hey, thanks. You're really lovely.'

'It's fine. I'm only doing it because I think you're really hot.'

I blushed.

When I got out of the shower, she was gone, and there was a ridiculous T-shirt lying on the bed. I grabbed a shopping bag from the kitchen drawer, stole a little of her hair product and moisturiser, packed up my book and crushed-up shirt, put the key in my pocket and hit the streets.

2000: AMY

They tell me I shouldn't wear heels any more, that my ankles are fat and swollen enough now without the extra pressure of heels. But hey, if you can't wear your best boots, what's the point in going on?

My tummy, as predicted, has swollen to a size where Prada rip-offs just aren't an option anymore. So I'm all in stretchy black and non-stretchy leather, and wearing my dark red Italian boots, which don't go with anything I own and are as uncomfortable as hell. Plus, of course, there's the stump issue. I look ridiculous. I look ridiculous and I don't care anymore, don't give a damn. Since the ambulance took me away from you there hasn't been a whole lot of point in looking attractive anyway. I don't want anyone to look at me.

And sitting here I'm surrounded by women who are doing the whole 'glowing from the inside' thing, all of them blonde, shiny and irritating as fuck. Meanwhile, I've got two inches of mousy regrowth and the doctor tells me if I use so much as a teaspoon of burgundy hair dye the poison will probably kill the baby. I'd been given to believe that the pregnancy gig was supposed to make one smugly calm, angelically self-possessed; you know, as if one's womb were, like, the centre of the universe and one were the holder of all secrets of said universe. Mostly I just feel grumpy, like slapping the smugly calm faces of just about everyone in my prenatal class. Look at them all, in their flowing, wistful cotton, their silky ponytails in banana clips. I swear, if god gave me one wish, it'd be to see every banana clip – and perhaps every head of hair ever held up by a banana clip – burning on a giant, gasoline-soaked inferno. All that plastic melting into one hideous lump.

God, I'm irritable.

'Ms Crawford?'

I haul my fat arse out of the plastic chair and into the doctor's office.

'Hi. Have a seat. So, how are you feeling?'

Blah, blah, blah . . . blood pressure, urine samples, ultrasounds, questions about diet, questions about my mental well-being . . .

'And how's the father coping?'

You tell me. But I guess he means Derek.

'He's fine.'

Is he fine? I don't know. We don't talk about any of this. He knows this baby is nothing to do with him, but he never even mentions that. He's quiet, he's there when I need him – to lift things, to help me out of the car – never asks about our future, never angry with me, never asks about our past. He pretty much doesn't give a damn about me or the baby or anything, except in as much as we're his fellow human beings, and he's a decent guy. Maybe it's his British upbring-ing – that stiff upper lip nonsense. He's been working night-shift a lot, spending a lot of time at the hospi-tal, so we don't see that much of each other. I spend a lot of time sitting in the armchair, looking at cats on the fire escapes and watching the rain on the window, wrapped in a blanket. It's been cold.

According to the doctor, everything is hunky dory and as it should be. So that's something.

I go downstairs and get into my car. Driving has become an ordeal. The steering wheel causes discom-fort. In fact, pretty much everything, bar nothing, is pissing me off. How the hell am I going to snap out of this? God, I feel fat.

Once again, as always, you are singing on the radio. I change the station, but you're in my head now, like some kind of ear-dwelling urban-legend spider; spider thoughts are breeding in my brain. You know what? You loved my ass and my laugh and the way I made you sound like a genius. But me, I could barely breathe without you, and you wanted none of that. A smarter woman would have written you off as fun, hot and well-and-truly a long-term terrible idea, but instead I dream about you every single night. Every night you're there in my dreams, and in my dreams we don't fight and you don't yell at me and we don't even have eye-boggling sex in luxurious hotel hot-tubs. We just sit still. We sit still and you hold my hand, and sometimes you lean over to me and whisper something in my ear, and I can feel your warm breath on my cheek, and I don't hear the words at all, but I know they're kind. So every morning when I wake up I'm calm, happy, content. And all of two minutes later a damp, grey blanket – it's mildewy, too, this blanket, and smells of mould – slaps into my frontal lobe and that's it for me and calm happiness for the rest of the day. Cause here I am, and there you are, and even if we were in the same place you would probably dance for me, strip for me, buy me cocktails and sexy bras but you would never once sit still and hold my hand and speak kindly to me. And maybe, just maybe, if I tried just a little bit to be a good wife, Derek would, but I can't, so he doesn't. And I'm full of baby, and it's your baby and that's impossible, but what other explanation is there? And I hope she has your curly hair. And I hope I don't drown her in my stupid, lost, hopeless tears. I hope I can find space in my brain to even notice her.

Shit.

Ah, home, sweet home. Groceries left on the bench because I just don't have the energy to put them away. Dishes in the sink: ditto. Newspaper open on the coffee table, our squashy little living room, three coffee cups of differing fullness, half-empty beer bottle, open CD cases strewn on the floor. I put 'Emotional Rescue' on the stereo, slump on the couch and flick listlessly through the paper. Oh look, what a surprise. Turns out that the whole image-change thing was a great idea: your nationwide tour of deco theatres and tasteful dive bars is selling fast and you're playing here, live in concert. Joy. And a week after I'm due too: maybe I'll take the baby to meet her pa.

Leave me the hell alone, will you?

So I distract myself with tidying the apartment. Do the dishes, sweep the floor, *mop* the floor, for Christ's sake. Rearrange the bookshelf. Pick up the CD covers, put the CDs back in the CD covers, contemplate putting the CDs in alphabetical order, go for colour-coding instead, note that we have more black-spined CDs, by far, than any other coloured spine, curse the spineless spine designers, sit on the couch and cry.

I want to see you. I want to see you so bad. Like acid reflux, this constant aching in my solar plexus from the wanting of you. Like swallowing a corn chip the wrong way down, but to the power of five; like my trachea has been stuffed with hessian. Without you, this city is heartbreaking. There, the cinema where we watched that ridiculous fashionista art flick; there, the corner where a fan complimented you on your choice of pizza; that café, where you told me a story which involved the inadvertent admission that one morning, the week before, I'd been the first thing you'd thought of when you woke up; the goddamn bar where I bit your lip that night. The impossibility of you with me, the inevitability of losing you but still, the feeling that without you my life has taken a terrible wrong turn into irrelevancy. Who is living my real life, there with you?

And I tell myself I won't but I know first thing Saturday morning I'll be downtown lining up for a ticket. And hating myself every single second of every minute of the five hours I'll stand in that line. And that being no different to how I feel right now.

2000: BENJAMIN

They told her she's almost better. They said she could go home soon.

She wasn't all that excited. Mainly because she didn't have a home in this city anymore, because seven weeks in hospital, not working, is really way too long to be paying rent on a house where you weren't even living. So she hadn't been. So now she had no home.

So, imagine: she didn't have a home and she didn't have a job. She did have a bunch of medical bills. She suspected that, as the accident happened on board a piece of municipal transport, and as the driver of said transport was found at fault, the government probably owed her a shitload of money but she didn't really know how to go about getting any of it. So, overall, the prospect of leaving this quiet, white womb where her every need was catered for and all she had to deal with was the paralysing boredom wasn't looking that hot.

Plus, the upside of hanging around this hospital for, say, the term of her natural life was that person who visited her almost every day. He was the person who, she supposed, had saved her life. He was a nurse, a nurse from this very hospital; the nurse who had stopped the bleeding, and called the ambulance, and read to her while she lay unconscious. And she had to admit she was a little smitten: his English accent, his crooked English teeth, his oversized hands. And it wasn't just that he had a calming voice and big hands: he was also freaking hot, she reminded herself. He had the narrowest butt. She really wanted to bite it. She really wanted to bite it while he was reading her a story.

Her arm was almost healed. Except, of course, it wasn't her arm anymore. So strange, so strange after 22 years to have a part of her that's not her. See, this, her right hand. She remembered the time she had picked up a spider, a spider sitting on a brick, with this right hand, taken the brick to her dad to ask him what the creature was, seen the fear in his eyes while he said, 'oh look, isn't it cute. Give it to me, now, sweetheart.' And she remembered this right hand, this one here and the time she had used it to smash her little brother's head into the living room wall when he wouldn't let her watch TV. The time her right hand forgot how to play piano in front of 300 people; the time it sliced her left wrist up with a shiny new razorblade and she was happily surprised at the inverse relationship between pain and blood (and wondered where the scars from that incident were now that her left arm was somewhere entirely elsewhere); the time she ran the fingers of that right hand over the shifting texture of sideburn, cheek, sideburn (and how hard it was to choose between the two as far as what the fingertips of her right hand most wanted to be touching at that time).

And for the left hand? Nothing. Nothing at all.

Anyway, the skin grafts joining what had always been her arm to what would, from now on be her arm, were almost healed. The skin was creepily different on the lower half of her left arm to what it was on the upper half; paler above, darker below.

She missed her old left hand, felt a weird guilt for abandoning it, letting it die before the rest of her did. And without knowing where it was buried, if indeed it was buried at all. She assumed it wasn't: surely if it had been in any state for burial, they would have reconnected it to her elbow rather than hooking her up to this stranger's limb. It must have been mashed. Perhaps they smushed it up with all the other leftover fleshy bits and pieces: the unattachables, the unclaimed extremities, the bits that, had you put them together, would have made whole humans, and just incinerated the lot of them.

Poor old left hand: never up for much, kind of uncoordinated, couldn't catch a ball, slapdash and next-to-useless for handjobs, couldn't write upside down with it but better than most right-handers' left hands when it came to arm wrestles, nifty on a keyboard, carried its weight during shoulder massages, just fine for scratching under a right scapula. Good, perhaps better even than the right hand, for delicate little-finger ferreting around in a nostril. Gone now, and no sooner gone than callously replaced (without her say-so, she'd like to add, particularly if left arm is somewhere asking about such things; done while she was heavily anaesthetised and entirely without her knowledge). Superseded, and by a new left arm that was, she'd been led to believe, more attractive: certainly her new left fingernails didn't have the propensity to split and flake which the old ones had had. She had been an unwilling accomplice in the betrayal of her very own limb.

'What are you frowning at?'

The sun came out, the clouds evaporated; guilt became nothing more than a residual rime in the corners of her subconscious. Forgotten as quickly as she'd forgotten her left arm, a tiny fraction of her subconscious chided her.

'Hi.'

'Hi. What's up?' Derek asked her.

'I was just thinking about my old arm. Wondering where it's got to, if it's OK. My teddybear always promised me – and I promised him – that when I died we'd be buried together. We always assumed he wouldn't die first. I don't know if I should cut off Ted's left arm and bury it with mine. What do you think?'

'Technically not yet.'

'Sorry?'

'Not yet. Your arm is downstairs. They have to hang on to it. For the investigation – you know – into the crash.'

'Oh.' She was revolted, curious, sad and angry all at once. 'Really?'

'Really. It could be evidence. For compensation.'

'Can I have it back after?' She didn't know if she actually wanted it back but she definitely wanted to know if it was an option.

'I don't think so. They usually burn them afterwards.'

'Ah.' Still the same bundle of feelings and a brief desperate urge to run down to the basement, rescue her arm and flee the hospital. She didn't want Derek to think she was crazy or grim. Keep it light-hearted! 'So I should cut Ted's arm off and put it in the freezer?'

'Something like that,' he smiled. 'Or preserve it in a bottle.' Neither of them knew what to say next. Benjamin stared at her new arm for a while.

'Anyway,' Derek burst out, 'they tell me you're getting out in a couple of days.'

'That's the word on the wards.'

'I guess you're not altogether thrilled.'

'Not really.'

'Well, if it helps I put a notice up for you on the

board downstairs and I've signed you up for a couple of online rental agencies.'

'You rule.'

Derek had opened the cupboard by her bed, looking for the book he'd been reading to her. 'I don't really want you to go,' he said, head still mostly buried in the cupboard.

'You don't?' she wanted him to keep talking but was suddenly a little nervous of what he might say.

'How will I fill in all the hours I usually spend watching you sleep?' This time he looked her right in the eye.

'You watch me sleep?' she asked.

'You talk sometimes. I've been waiting to hear your secrets.' He sat down and opened *The English Patient*.

She hoped he was joking. She hoped he wasn't joking. She was suddenly horribly frustrated by this ugly gown, this drip, these bandages. She wanted a cocktail and a cigarette and dim lighting and the chance to find out just how far he was really prepared to take this.

'He has been disassembled by her,' Derek said. He paused, looked down again at the page. 'You remember?'

She remembered. He began reading.

'What day is it?' she interrupted.

'Saturday.' And quieter, 'it's Saturday, darling.'

She let the whispered endearment pass by without

comment. 'In that case, can we watch football?'

He closed the book and placed it on the floor, rubbed his hand over his eyes. He smiled at her, suddenly sunny.

'It's not football,' he told her.

See, she thought: he isn't that serious. 'Is too,' she said.

'Is not.'

'Is too.'

'Is not. Where's the feet?'

'There's feet. They're just a little intermittent, is all . . .'

'Whatever.'

But he let go of her hand – the hand he had been surreptitiously holding as though his hand and his brain were operating independently of one another – and turned on the television. Then he went down to the cafeteria to stock up on Coke and Kettle chips, which she was strictly forbidden by hospital ruling to eat in bed but upon which he gladly turned a blind eye.

When he came back she was shouting under her breath, if such a thing is possible.

'No, nuh, oh, Jesus CHRIST! Are you a freaking MORON? You KNOW he can't catch for shit; why did you pass it to him? JESUS!'

'You OK there?'

'Oh god, this guy is such a MORON. If he's not passing it to some dickwad who's never caught a ball in his life, he's STANDING there THINKING about running and not THROWING until he gets his stupid dickwaddish face slammed into the turf. I don't know why I bother.'

'Because you do – don't you? Hard work for you, there, propped up on four pillows.'

'Ah, fuck you.'

He smiled.

'What?'

He smiled again and she saw that look return to his eyes.

'Pff. Fuck you.' She blushed; she felt herself blush. 'Look. No, stupid, over there; at the TV. Look! He's doing it again!'

'Of course he is.'

But this time he actually did look.

She fell asleep in the third quarter. The guys in turquoise were up 24 points on the guys in grey, and even he could tell it wasn't a game anymore.

2000: AMY

It's cold, cold, cold, and the rain has finally stopped. The shadows are long but I've angled myself so the sun is on my back, and even through the long-sleeved T-shirt, the pullover and the suede jacket (which won't do up over my insane belly), the skin between my shoulder blades is feeling like a stretching kitten's tummy in a beam of warm light.

The guy next to me in the line is dressed like a Vietnam vet: dark blue bomber jacket with some sort of schizophrenic pro-and-anti-American patch sewn on it, torn jeans, bandana, aviator sunglasses – just the right age. Apparently a homeless Vietnam vet: he's covered in grime, his teeth are brown and sparse and he has a vague odour – that strange smell of stale socks and old snot common to teenage boys. When I first got in line I thought he was just some crazy guy hanging around but it turned out that, despite appearance and regardless of whatever other problems he was having re personal hygiene, he'd scraped together the cash to get himself a ticket for your show. I'm not sure what's dragged him here, whether he's got his heart set on hearing you belt out the patriotic glory-rock tracks you cashed in on before you went alternative, or whether it's the post-divorce, morally edgy version that gets him pumped. Maybe he just likes your gorgeous smile.

After waiting here about two hours, making a little friendly chit chat about this and that, a friend of the veteran's turns up to give him some company. The friend is about three feet tall, very loud, and also has a red bandana tied around his head. He's been chatting away to everyone in the line, keeping us entertained, and he was smart enough to bring his own seat. Every now and again, he lets me have a turn sitting on it – the cripple and the fat lady pooling their resources.

All day, passers-by and tourists stop to ask what we're lining up for. Most of them have a pet theory; all of them are happy to share their pet theory with anyone who'll listen. 'Must be someone signing autographs. Who's signing autographs?' 'Why are you so desperate for football tickets? Is this some kind of special game?'

And now, this woman, another passer-by, stops to ask us a few more inane questions. She's a classy-looking lady, late 50s, dressed in a business suit and a red turtleneck, pulling one of those wheely suitcases behind her. 'What are you waiting for?' she asks, somewhat predictably. Someone tells her we're wait-ing to buy tickets for your show.

'Who's she? Huh?' she snaps. 'I've never heard of her.'

Our pal the helpful dwarf says (loudly, because she seems a little hard of hearing, and just because he's a loud kind of guy), 'She's a musician, ma'am. A MUSICIAN.'

'You don't have to yell, little man.' She turns on her heel and drags her suitcase off after her.

He mutters something under his breath about there being no need to overreact and – surprise, surprise – she hears that and storms right on back.

'What did you say?'

'I was just telling you she's a musician.'

'Listen to me, you funny-looking little mother-fucker. You might think you're a bad-ass, but I'll show you who's a fucking bad-ass!'

She's pulling something out from under her tai-lored blazer. It's a Fed-Ex envelope, and she's waving it above her head in an effort to guarantee each of us will get a look at it. 'I'll show you who's a bad-ass!'

The envelope is fat with documents, papers poking out at all sorts of angles, in some sort of filing system apparent only to her. She tugs one out and shoves it in his face. It's covered in tiny, tiny writing, min-iature black-inked block capitals. At the bottom, HOMELESS is penciled, huge and uppercase.

'See this?' she's yelling. 'See this? This is the instructions for the neutron bomb! I gave 'em to the Red Chinese! That's right – now you're scared, aren't you? I'll show you who's a bad-ass, you midget mother-fucker!'

She shoves the paper back in the envelope and sets off down the street again, the suitcase tipping over from side to side and significantly impeding her furious progress. How can we help but laugh? There we all are, bonded together in snickers.

For a minute it looks like she's going to come back but instead she yells over her shoulder, 'don't mess with me! I could give them the fusion bomb as well!'

Even if I don't get the tickets, I think, the day will be far from wasted.

And then, when it comes, it isn't anything like it is on TV. I don't gasp, don't suck in my breath or claw at my belly. Contractions, they call them, but for me it's more like a sliding, like a subatomic displacement. An almost supernatural discomfort that doesn't leave me crying or urgent but rather makes the skin on my back prickle with its complete unfamiliarity. Something is in me, and it's shifting.

'Oh.'

I knew what it was, of course, knew I should 'take steps'. But it's made me insane, this thing with you; not insane in a poetic way. I'm not talking metaphors here; I'm actually incapable of operating like a sane human being. So, in line with that, I'm in line. And there's no way I'm giving up my spot.

I can feel my jaw clicking out of place, the way I'm thrusting it forward with the concentrating. I'm determined to stick this out.

'Ah. Jesus!'

They don't ask, of course. They're all fucking insane too.

And it passes. And it comes back. And it passes. But it keeps coming back stronger: the shifting, the feeling like the bottom is dropping out of me. That, at least, is how I expected it to be: the waves of it, the ebb and flow of intensity.

'Your turn on the seat, ma'am.'

But I can't take it, can't take my mind off this for a second.

'Thanks, no.'

'Please. You should take the weight off.'

'Shh!'

'Are you alright?'

'SHUT UP PLEASE.'

'Um, ma'am, you don't look so good. Jim, she's not looking so good.'

Don't listen to them. Line's moving. Move with the line. Probably only five or six people in front of me now. Any minute; any minute. God, I didn't want this . . . didn't ask for this . . .

But I did want it, of course. Wanted the

swollen belly, wanted the braids, wanted the soft, sweet domesticity due to a woman in my condition. And instead, here I am, barely standing, but standing in a line for tickets for a fucking rock star who used to screw me, standing in the freezing cold – me, a grown woman with a goddamn baby squirming inside her and wondering when the fuck I'm going to grow up and get over all this. When does the part happen where I'm happy with my lot?

I feel myself unfolding, feel like balled gloves being unballed, the inside moving to the outside. And now it's not just the insides of me shifting but the street is shifting too, the building shifting, everything's on its side and I can hear a voice: 'See! See, Jim! I told you!'

2022: PAUL

So today it finally sank in. I'm dead.

Oh, you're thinking, it's like that film, the one where the guy was dead but they spent the whole film trying to disguise that he was dead but the whole way through he was a ghost and only the little kid could see him, and you only realise right at the very end.

OK, first off, this isn't the end; besides which, I told you from the very beginning I was dead so there are no surprises here for you. I'm surprised, sure, but you have no reason to be.

Second, I'm not a ghost. So that's different too.

I called my bank this morning to ask what the deal was with my credit card. They claimed to have no record of me. Never heard of me, they said. Never had a customer with that ID number, sir, I'm sorry. I'm sorry, sir, but I just can't help you, I don't know what to suggest. Perhaps you'd like to open an account with us? The upside of which being, I guess, that at least I don't have to pay them back the $1300 I owe them.

In need of cash, nonetheless, I paid a visit to the

nearest ATM. Not surprisingly, though still disappointingly, the ATM was not at all interested in giving me cash and in the end swallowed my card. The machine advised me to call my bank for more information but I'm not so stupid that I hadn't twigged to the fact that that was going to be an almighty waste of time.

Undaunted, I made my way to the Identity Office, stopping only to shoplift a pen from a newsagent (a chain store; I have morals). Feeling like an old hand, I took a number, did the wait, got the form, filled in the form, took a number, did the wait and got the call.

'Good morning. This is my application form for unemployment assistance, filled in in pen.'

'Thank you Mr . . . Mr Crawford. You will hear from us in approximately two weeks. A notice will be mailed to you. Here is a sheet outlining our responsibilities and repeating the information which I have just given you.'

'OK, but I need some money now.'

'The form you have filled out does not entitle you to emergency assistance.'

'Can I have the form that does?'

'You'll have to take a number.'

'That all makes perfect sense to me and I can see why the system was instituted. Obviously you want everyone to be treated fairly. I can see that you wouldn't want difficult customers taking too much of your time as that would detract from the service experience of others waiting to be assisted.'

'Here's the form.'

'Thank you.'

I took a number and a seat. This form was a doddle. Name, address (I put it down, even though I had no idea if it was still my address), phone, ID number, steps you're taking to alleviate your financial situation, assets, reasons you need the money.

Numbers passed, and mine was called.

'Good morning, how can I help you?'

'Hi. Did you miss me while I was gone?'

That wasn't a happy smile.

'This is my application for emergency assistance.'

'Alright, Mr Crawford. You'll have to speak to one of our client management officers. I'll pass this on to,' here she did a quick shuffle through some papers, 'Elizabeth Conathan, who will be with you in a moment. If you take a seat, your name will be called shortly.'

'Why, thank you.'

But it wasn't all that shortly. I saw a whole episode of *Death Row Mercy Call*, the new daytime reality TV show, plus half a rerun (for the 19th time) of *Sex & the City* before Ms Conathan cracked the door and called me in.

I got to sit in a proper chair in a proper office, opposite Ms Conathan's desk, which had her name on it.

'Mr Crawford, there seems to be a problem with your application.'

'It's in pen.'

'We're having trouble calling up information relating to your identity number.'

I looked simultaneously blank and fascinated.

'Central records show that the person holding this identity number died 12 days ago.'

'Ah. That sounds like a mistake.'

'It's not a mistake.'

'Hmm. Did you type it in right?'

'We've checked and rechecked. I have personally called head office and had this checked over the phone, and there's no mistake.'

'I'm not dead.'

'For our purposes, I'm afraid you are. I'm sorry, Mr Crawford, but we just can't help you. I don't know what to suggest.'

'Well, Ms Conathan, it seems we are at an impasse. If you could see your way clear to loaning me a hundred bucks or so I'll get out of your way and let you continue doing the bang-up job you're so obviously doing.'

'Don't make me call security.'

'Wouldn't dream of it.'

On my way out I handed my pen to a woman desperately rifling through her purse for what looked like the seventh time.

My cell phone still had a bit of credit left, so, just for the hell of it, I called work. I had them put me through to Louise.

'Hey, Louise. It's Paul Crawford here. How're you going? Things still rolling along alright without me?'

'Sorry, who did you say it was?'

'It's Paul, Louise. Remember. I worked there two weeks ago.'

'Oh, Paul, hi, how are you? How are you feeling? Are you OK?'

'Apparently I'm dead.'

'I know, they told us. I'm sorry. I'm really sorry, Paul.'

'Oh, it's OK. It's not as bad as I'd expected it to be.'

'Sorry, Paul. It's kind of a bad time. I was just on my way to weekly staff meeting. But you'd remember that.'

'Of course. You run along. And hey, say hi to the others for me.'

'Paul, you're dead. People don't like hearing hi from dead people. It makes them uncomfortable.'

Oh for fuck's sake. I hung up. I had enough money for a beer.

I spent some time standing at the bar we'd been at the other night, drinking slowly, slowly. Making it last. Enjoying being warm. Getting to the bottom of the glass, and then realising my options had narrowed to almost nil. I didn't want to, but I didn't know what else to do.

I pulled out my phone, dialled my dad.

'Derek Crawford speaking.'

'Hi Dad. It's me.'

'Paul! How are you?'

'Dad, I need some help.'

'What? What is it, Paulie? Are you OK?'

'Oh, I'm fine. Don't worry. It's just there's some weird stuff going on with my identity number, and . . .'

'What do you mean "weird stuff"?'

'Well, I seem to have been wiped from the records.'

'Oh. What does that mean, exactly?'

'Well, it kinda means I don't exist anymore. The bank won't give me any of my money, and work fired me, and I can't get Identity to help me, and now it looks like I've been kicked out of my house.'

I thought I'd been handling all this but now, with my dad there on the other end of the line, and hearing the dog grumbling into his hand while he rubs under her jaw and him going 'mmm, mmm, mmm' and actually really caring, I could hear it in his voice, I just found myself sobbing. I just wanted Dad to come down here and get me and make everyone stop being so mean to me.

Which, of course, he said he'd do. He said he'd pick me up out the front of my former residence in two hours. And so he told me he loved me, and I hung up, and now I'm here, sitting in the gutter out the front of my house, crying into my hands and people walking by me, and not one person even looking twice.

2000: AMY

When you were born, Paul, I was unconscious still. They got me to the hospital. They found my wallet and put me in a cab – no one sure if I'd be able to afford an ambulance, if I had insurance – and asked the driver to drop me at the hospital.

The orderlies picked me up from the back seat and checked me in without me ever waking up. The cab driver, it seemed, helped himself to a sizeable tip, which was also fair enough: I hadn't been much of a conversationalist. I imagine the registrar on the front desk had tried to get me to fill in those interminable forms despite my lack of consciousness.

By the time they got me to an operating theatre, my waters had broken but you were refusing to make an appearance. I suspect the doctor was operating outside his legal responsibilities when he decided to perform a Caesarian section on an unconscious woman without even attempting to find any next of kin, but I guess he, the doctor, probably had a golf game or some other cliché to attend to. So he took my dream of spiralling scars, a belly circled by a cobweb of white lines, took it and made it a knife-edged reality. I suppose it was for the best; it was certainly poetic, and that's the driving principle of the obstetric medical profession, I believe.

So there was no one there to witness your entry into the world, to cry tears of miraculous joy, to hold your head, kiss your face; no one to press you to their leaking nipples and reseal the bond just fresh broken. When I woke up I was stitched and flat, the belly that was supposed to have bought me a place in the sun stolen away from me, replaced with – I didn't know what they'd replaced it with. Just knew I wanted it back. Wanted another chance to make it what it what it should have been. Wanted the sitting, the gazing; wanted her head resting on our distended, outsized love; wanted the shared anticipation, wanted her here now, holding my hand and stroking our baby's curly head.

They told me you were a boy. I thought they were lying. It just hadn't occurred to me that you could be a boy. Why would you be? They told me I could see you in a few hours – that you were downstairs with all the other babies, in the glass box. But I didn't want to see you. And I didn't understand why they kept asking me if I did. You and I were over now, as far as I was concerned. You'd moved on.

I loved you, I did. I just hadn't had a chance to figure it out. I had so much other stuff to think about.

I kept going back over my life, and I couldn't work out how I'd gotten to this place. None of what I had hoped or planned – even the stuff I'd lived, none of it – had led me to this. It just seemed implausible that I would be living in a tiny apartment with a husband who, thankfully, had next to no interest in me; that I would be in love with a woman who was a thousand miles away and, anyway, probably never wasted a thought on me and was probably right now deep in the embrace of some beautiful young thing; that I was now the mother of a tiny little boy child, a little child I was expected to care for for the next 20 years, at least. None of it made any sense.

They brought you to me, eventually, when I showed no interest in getting out of my bed. And you were beautiful. You are beautiful. Of course you're beautiful, my tiny, baby boy. You are, as far as I can tell, and even though it makes not a lick of sense, hers.

Within a few hours of them extracting you from me, your dad showed up. Of course your dad showed up. He had no biological reason to, but he cares, your dad. And he cared about you; even cared a little bit about me. He pronounced you beautiful, too. And it was him that named you Paul, though he never told me why. He said there wasn't any particular reason, that he just liked the name. And for the first time, that day, he sat down with me and actually talked about the things that had come to pass. And he promised me that, while he had no guarantees for me (understandably), he'd be there for you for as long as you needed. Has he been, Paul? Don't know why I'm asking: of course he has been.

Sorry to leave things like this, Paul. I'm sorry for all of it.

2000: DEREK

She had checked out.

He came in that morning, and she had checked out.

'Oh, she checked out late yesterday,' they told him.

'Oh, alright. Thanks,' he said. And for a while he believed it. The first two or three minutes, he continued on the trajectory he'd plotted before hearing the news. He went into the bathroom and put on his stretchy cap, setting it at a slightly jaunty angle, checking his reflection and remembering the compliments she'd given him on the curl his lengthening hair was developing. He came back out and checked the roster, established his schedule for the morning. He called the elevator and pressed the button for the seventh floor, where he was expected. And before he could check himself, pressed the button for the third floor as well, planning a slight detour to the floor where she should be, right now, eating an appalling breakfast concoction from a tray on her lap and watching TV. Only she wasn't. She wasn't there. Because she'd checked out and she hadn't told him, and he had no idea where she'd gone.

Why the fuck hadn't she told him she was leaving?

He stood in the elevator, by himself, and the doors to the third floor opened and he stood there, stock still, stood and stared at the floor where she should be, as the realisation of the days of her absence stretched before him. There was no reason he would ever see her again. He was not going to see her, not ever again. He ran the sentence through his mind, tried it in all its different forms, but it refused to settle there. He could feel it pounding against the very outer membrane of his brain, the unarguable statement that this was it: that he would not be seeing her ever again on his morning rounds, but it wouldn't quite permeate. He stood still staring while the door closed and the elevator continued upward. He got out on the seventh floor and headed for the ward, feeling like he'd forgotten something. And found, at the last minute, that he had to go to the bathroom again. Found that he had to lock himself in a stall because he was feeling sick from fury.

She'd fucking gone, and she hadn't fucking told him where. She hadn't FUCKING told him WHERE she was going. Was this any way to treat a friend? Weren't they friends? When he'd been sitting there, the day before, next to her bedside, holding her goddamn hand, hadn't it occurred to her that he might want to know if she was maybe thinking that later that day she might just head off? Had that not, perhaps, crossed her mind at the point where he'd said, 'Righto, Benjamin, I'll see you tomorrow, then'. Could she, perhaps, have said, 'Actually, I won't see you tomorrow, because I'm checking out. But don't worry, we can have a drink on the weekend. Perhaps you and I could go for a drink and, well, later, afterwards, perhaps we'll sleep side by side and I'll hold your hand all night and this time I'll tell *you* stories; while you're sleeping there, in my bed, with my arm across your chest and my fingers in your hair. Here's my phone number. Here's where I'll be. Because I don't ever want to be away from you.'

Fuck her. FUCK her.

He washed his face, thinking fuck her, fuck her, fuck her, who needs her, if it means so little to her, who needs her. Washed his face and splashed some water into his eyes, tried to wash away the red, thought that maybe he should go by the dispensary and get some eye drops. But perhaps he didn't need them, because he wasn't crying, because he was angry. Not scared, or abandoned; not shamed, or unneeded, unnecessary: he was angry. Fucking furious; he was fucking furious, in fact.

He walked back onto the ward. He was a professional. He knew his job, and he took his work seriously. He applied himself. And every two minutes, three minutes at the most, he thought again that he was going to call her and tell her how angry he was with her, demand an apology, and every two minutes, three minutes at the most, he remembered that he couldn't. And he was so preoccupied that when his break came around and he could stare, again, at the burnished stainless steel interior of a bathroom stall, let his face assume the expressions his brain had been demanding all morning, he didn't even have the presence of mind to be grateful that he hadn't managed to kill anyone.

When the front desk called him, at around three on that Saturday afternoon; when he picked up the phone to be told that he was a father, that his wife had had a Caesarian some hours ago, that he should come down to maternity and see his son, he was, for seconds at a time, entirely displaced. Wife? SON?

He went, though. Because that was the sort of thing he did. And as a result, here he was now, twenty-two years later, sitting in the car outside the house of the son of his former wife. Wife. They'd never divorced. And there, on the steps, sitting in a coat and what appeared to be, for no apparent reason, a Panthers football T-shirt, with curls breaking away from his pompadour and his face a little puffy from held-back tears, the first spark of recognition reorganising his face from bleak abandonment into competent cheer, was that son, the sweet child of his life if not his loins, his boy Paul.

2022: PAUL

'Hi Dad.'

'Are you OK?'

'Yeah, I'm fine. Thanks, Dad. Thanks for coming all this way.'

'Don't be silly. There seems to be some sort of drama around your house. What's up with the police tape?'

'Oh, Dad. I don't know.'

I got up from the stairs, grabbed my shopping bag and headed over to the car. 'The notice,' I pointed, 'on the door says the police are "conducting an investigation" but I called the number after I talked to you, and it's not real. Not a real number. It's disconnected. I guess it's my landlord's idea of a trouble-free eviction.'

'Should I call your landlord?'

'Dad, I haven't really been paying my rent.'

'Right. Well then, let's just pop in and get some of your things, shall we?'

'Do you think that's a good idea?'

'I think it'd be fine. I don't think fake police can arrest us.'

A little shaming, to have a dad less bowed by authority than one's self.

We were there about half an hour, all up, packing things in suitcases and a backpack. No one had painted toy dogs on the wall in blood.

We headed out of the city, leaving steep and narrow city streets behind for strip-mall-lined freeway, jazz on the stereo, Miles Davis I was guessing. The window cracked and I felt my face, in the wind, shedding old cells, laying in new ones.

'So, aside from all this, how *are* you, Paulie? Seeing anyone?'

'Not really.'

'What happened with that girl Greta? The girl at work? Weren't you two, um, dating for a while?'

'Not really. It didn't really work out.' Dad's too sharp; I've got to watch what I say around him. 'I did go for a drink with someone last night.'

'Uh huh.' That's the sound of Dad pretending not to sound too interested, but interested enough to keep me talking.

'She was nice, a very nice girl. She let me stay over at her place – no, Dad, not like that – when I couldn't get back into my place.'

'Someone from work?'

'I don't go to work, remember. Nope, someone in line with my exciting new life. I met her at the Identity Office.'

'There's nothing wrong with that. So, does she have a name?'

I couldn't tell my dad I'd been attempting to shag a girl called Benjamin.

'Bennie. I think it's short for Brenda.'

'That's a nice name.'

'Mmm. Don't know if I'll get to see her again, though. Oh, shit!' A look. 'Sorry. It's just I've got her key. Got the key to her house. She gave it to me this morning in case I couldn't find anywhere to stay.'

'If you don't mind me asking, is that T-shirt hers?'

'Yeah. Of course it is. It's a football T-shirt, Dad.'

He and I have been dealing with this for 22 years now: his obsessive love of football, despite the fact he has never had a team and my total lack of interest. He tried to teach me to pass, to tackle, when I was a kid and I gave it a shot, got good enough to hold my own with the next-door neighbour kids but given the choice I'd always much rather have been inside reading. I was such a disappointing child.

'She sounds nice.'

Dad is such a sucker.

'Perhaps you'd better give her a call, then, when we get home, so you can let her know you're OK. I can always drive you back into town to drop off her stuff later, if you like.'

'Or I can get the train, Dad. You don't have to drive me.'

'Ah. You're a big kid now, right?'
'You bet.'

2000: BENJAMIN

'You see,' she had imagined herself telling him, 'your wife is pregnant, in case you don't remember. Your child is about to be born.'

She wished two things. First, she wished no one had ever told her, that she'd never discovered the fact of his wife and imminent child. Of course, she didn't really, didn't want them to have unspoken things between them, especially not things that big. But imagine the bliss of never knowing . . . And second, she wished that, now knowing, she hadn't cared.

But she knew, and she cared. So next, she would have said, 'So I have to leave. We can't go on like this. I'm falling in love with you, and that's wrong. It will only end in pain for both of us. Goodbye.'

And a noble tear would have stood in her eye, perhaps fallen just as she turned her head, and he would have been left standing there, looking at the tear as it lay glistening on the hospital floor. Of course, he would have tried to follow her, would have cried out, told her – not caring who heard – that he loved her, that nothing else mattered, that his wife and child were as dust compared to the great love he held for her. But she would have been strong. She wouldn't have looked back. And for years afterwards, probably forever, he would have held that memory close to him, thought of her always as that brave, strong woman, that noble woman of high principles, for whom a corner of his heart would always be reserved. And he would never have had sex with his wife again, and he would have built a small shrine to her in a kitchen cupboard, and the baby would be named after her, and eventually he would find her but it would be too late because she would have died, tragically, just months before, and . . .

Instead, when she got a call from her dad's cousin offering her a room in her house for a few months, she just packed her stuff and left. She didn't feel much like crying in front of anyone right now. And deep down, though she didn't even really like to admit it to herself, it was a little bit creepy how much attention this married man, this soon-to-be new father, was paying to a bed-ridden girl he'd only just met. She thought about leaving a note for him at the desk but in the end she couldn't think of anything to say.

Three things, actually: she wished she knew his last name. You know, just in case. For later. In case she decided after all it was a good idea.

And now, living here in this attic room with its

big soft bed and lemon-yellow walls, she spent her days talking to lawyers, looking through rental listings, going to job interviews – a cosy little cocoon of bureaucracy and lists, all of which kept her from wondering about anything too much.

Her arm, meanwhile, was healing nicely. The interloper was trying harder to fit in these days, assimilating well with the rest of her limbs; the colour, chameleonic, blending itself with the rest of her skin.

She was still scared of it. She was scared of this lump of flesh – this stick of skin and bone that had been, however briefly, dead – couldn't help thinking of it as a parasite, an alien parasite. She worried if the rest of her body resented it, if her heart was bitter about having to pump blood to this foundling child, if the whole thing might one day rebel on her, leave her. If one day she'd wake up to discover the rest of her body had abandoned her, left her there with just her new arm and a note that read, 'If you like it so damn much, why don't you look after it?'. She wasn't quite sure what 'she' would constitute once she'd been abandoned by her body, but, still, it was worth worrying about.

Where had it come from, this arm? Whose damn arm was it anyway? She'd been so preoccupied with worrying about what had happened to her old arm, preoccupied with, let's face it, Derek, that she'd never really asked, never tried to find out who'd been kind enough to donate their unwanted arm to her.

She assumed it had been unwanted. And sometimes that made her feel a bit sorry for the arm.

She'd mentioned it to Derek a couple of times, obliquely. As in, 'Hey, Derek, where the hell did this arm come from, then?' and he'd suggested that she should be grateful for small mercies, quit asking so many questions and pass him the chips. Which she had done.

She couldn't help feeling he was avoiding the subject, sweeping something under the rug, as it were. Usually so voluble, he tended to cut any conversations regarding the arm a little bit short, if you'll pardon the pun. Not in a mean way, of course – Derek was never mean – just in a slightly over-efficient British way. It had crossed her mind a few times that perhaps she should make a few inquiries herself, circumvent her nursing pal and go straight to the source. But there always seemed to be something better to do. And now it was too late. Now she was trying to ensure that, as far as the hospital was concerned, she didn't exist. As for what had happened to *her* arm, the arm she'd grown up with and grown somewhat fond of, she'd been advised by the hospital counselor to 'let it go'. She'd snorted a bit when he'd said that.

So sometimes, when she had a quiet moment in between cheerfully representing herself to solicitors, human resources managers, real estate agents, client relations coordinators and so forth, she'd sit still and let her new arm tell her a few stories about its past. It was important, she felt, that they spend this quiet time together. It wasn't just up to the arm to do all the work, all the assimilating; she needed to try to understand where the arm was coming from too, to make some allowances for its memories and culture.

'So arm, what's up?' she'd ask it.

And if she lay back on the bed, the big soft bed between the lemon-yellow walls, the square of sunlight from the high-up window falling across her calves, whispers of thoughts of hints of memories would travel up through her veins and to the space between her eyes.

. . . sitting alone in a cold room, a dimly lit bathroom, sitting alone in the gigantic empty bathtub . . . I don't even remember being introduced to her. But I remember the first time I noticed how soft the hairs on her arm were. And I remember the first time I saw that the blue of her eyes was not the same. I remember her chewing gently on my bottom lip, I remember her forehead wrinkling at my tears, I remember her voice sticky with sleep, I remember the way her jaw tightened as her neck arched back. I remember her fingers rubbing my skull and her softness when she told me that was reason enough to live. I don't remember when I first saw her, but I remember when I knew . . . in a café, watching a woman over her breakfast, trying to concentrate on the conversation, thoughts louder than the words

. . . the ceiling, the ceiling in the light of a late afternoon, shadows long . . . The first warm afternoon of spring. The clouds break and we lie draped on the bed, soaking up the sunshine angled across the sheet. It's really too cold to be naked but we're dreaming of summer. My fingers lounge in the softness of her belly and she flinches gently – reflexes – as they drop lazily down to her thigh. She smells lovely and I want to taste her skin, but the sunshine suggests that days like this last forever, so I put it off a little longer . . . I want to breastfeed you like a baby, to hold your fragile newborn head, to know you as you were when you were fresh and wondering and alive. I want to lick the salty sweetness from your body, suck the bitterness from your soul, taste your hunger in my mouth, breathe the universe over your tongue. I want to dive into the depths of you and come up with pearls between my teeth . . .'

This afternoon it was a different dream, one she hadn't had before. Like trying to pick up mercury, grasping hold of this dream as the day reasserted itself. There were flowers, a bunch of poppies in brown paper, and a man's voice, familiar – really, really familiar – reading from what sounded like a shopping list and laughing. But it left her, became an artist's interpretation of a memory rather than the memory itself, so she got up.

'Akiko?'

The house was quiet.

'Akiko, are you around?'

Apparently not. She had left a note on the kitchen table saying she'd be home for dinner. Akiko, her father's cousin, had migrated from Kobe more than twenty years ago, found a Japanese-American husband, lost him again. Now, with her daughter grown and moved up north, she spent her days running the library at the local elementary school and her nights watching Masterpiece Theatre or at her weekly quilting circle. Akiko worried. She worried about whether Benjamin would find a house, find a job, worried about how she was going to live, worried that she'd never get a husband what with her horrific, deforming scars (she'd never said this to Benjamin, of course, but Benjamin had caught her drift), forced her to show up to her endless medical and legal appointments which Benjamin would just as soon have skipped, at least sometimes. She'd have liked a little more time for reading a book in the park in the sun, for example; a little more time for programming jukeboxes, a little more time for flirting with bartenders, a little more time for sitting on a bench in the museum staring at one picture for 23 minutes, just to throw out the statisticians' figures on art viewing. Oh, she had plans. Big plans.

But right now, her plan was to eat this apple on the way to the bus stop. Despite everything, including her own expectations, she had not developed a pathological fear of public transport. She could still squash onto a bus, holding on to a slippery, human-grease-lubricated stainless steel pole with two fingertips quite happily while being thrown almost off her feet at every sharp corner. Sometimes she had to force herself to remember what it had felt like, what the crash had felt like, just to make sure she was still a functioning human being, that she hadn't sublimated the whole thing, stuck it in some deep, dark place where later, at an inopportune moment (meeting her future parents-in-law, she suspected) it would leap forth and make her into a gibbering, dribbling maniac. But that didn't seem to be the case: she remembered the whole thing perfectly clearly but none of it had any resonance for her. It just didn't throw a decent emotional punch.

Her plan was to eat this apple, make it in time for the 2.17 71 bus and head downtown for a job interview.

She'd applied for a job in her field – dioramas – and she'd been eminently well qualified so she'd gotten an interview. But instead of going to the museum where the job would be, she had to go to some corporate office downtown, dress up like a freak, and talk about how marvellously skilled she was, rather than getting a chance to prove it. So be it: she assumed they must know what they were doing.

The interview was a breeze. Anyone with two brain cells to rub together could handle these things – smile, look confident, meet their eyes, think on the fly, ask questions back. The interviewer complimented her on her suit. The interviewer shook her hand and told her they'd be speaking again in the next few days. The interviewer had been trained in shaking hands.

The whole thing had gone both smoothly and quickly and she was feeling hopeful. In fact, she felt good enough about it that it didn't seem unreasonable to start looking at some places to live. She had a feeling she'd soon have enough incoming to pay a bit of rent.

She grabbed a set of keys from a one-man outfit run by a chap who had a touch of the Baltic about him. He called her sweetie, which didn't worry her, while she filled out the deposit receipt and handed over her ID card (she didn't have a driver's licence, which was a perpetual and recurring pain in the ass) and gave him her best smile. He agreed to let her keep the keys overnight, what with it now being 4.45pm, provided she left a slightly more sizeable deposit and promised that she'd be on the doorstep of the office, keys in hand, when he showed up in the morning.

The little apartment was on her bus line, which was nice. She'd grown quite fond of this neighbourhood on her travels through it over the past few weeks. It had two levels of front door: a big wrought iron door and a glass-paned one behind it. The stairs up to the third floor were narrow and steep, carpeted and clean. Someone had put a big potted plant on the first landing, and even bothered to water it. The apartment behind door 37 was tiny but it had rooms, and she knew that was something to be grateful for. The bedroom was at least partially partitioned from the living room with a door that actually closed; the tiny kitchen had no door but it did have a door frame. The bathroom really was one, with a bath. She thought that she probably liked it.

The power wasn't on and it was getting dark. 'Screw it,' she thought, 'I'm going to stay.' She dumped her bag and walked the three blocks to Akiko's house, where Akiko was still not home, changed into jeans and a T-shirt, big boots and a suede coat. She grabbed a comb and a toothbrush and some toothpaste, a blanket and a pillow, her book and a notebook and a pencil, shoved them all in a bag, left Akiko a note to the effect that she would be staying at a friend's place and headed back to the apartment. Dropped everything except her book and her wallet and the keys right in the geometric centre of the living room floor and skipped back downstairs.

There had to be somewhere to eat around here. Two blocks down the hill, one to the right, there was a tiny Italian restaurant, cheap enough to be plausible. She ordered vegetarian lasagna and a glass of red wine, and sat back with her book feeling pretty damn proud of herself. This was going to be good. This was all working out just fine.

Back at the apartment, opening the second of the two front doors and a little drunk, she saw a man stopped on the stairs. He stared, just a second, then passed her by without looking up. She thought perhaps he was wearing a wig.

She'd bought candles at the corner store and she set them up on windowsills and the mantelpiece (something else to be thankful for) and lit them all. She sat still, sitting inside herself. Alone. She could hear Derek talking to her and asked him to please be quiet. She didn't feel ready to talk to him just yet. She was having a new life.

When she'd blown the candles out and tried her best to get comfortable on the carpet, under her purple blanket, she noticed the rain on the window, thought about what it must be like to hear rain on the roof, wondered if she'd ever have a house of her own, one with a roof.

And in between the rain, the noise of the rain, and the sound of a stereo somewhere, and her own sleepy thoughts, was a voice, an accented voice, talking – reading? – to itself.

This is an unexpected climax, after all. I didn't expect this. What are you all standing up for, gentlemen? Sit down; congratulate me and the prince! Ferdishenko, just step out and order some more champagne, will you? 'Katia, Pasha,' she added suddenly, seeing the servants at the door, 'come here! I'm going to be married, did you hear? To the prince. He has a million and a half of rou-bles; he is Prince Muishkin, and has asked me to marry him. Here, prince, come and sit by me; and here comes the wine. Now then, ladies and gentlemen, where are your congratulations?'

The pulse in her wrist – her new wrist – was flut-tering and fast. Impossible as it seemed, her old arm's pulse stayed smooth and slow. She had begun falling into a dream and it was like the dream had been sit-ting waiting for her. She almost heard it say, 'Finally; you're here'. In the dream Derek was there and she could see her hands reaching out to him, him in a suit, he looked beautiful. He was squeezing her hand, her pulse quickening again, and she could hear someone else talking to them, knew it was important . . .

Her last waking thought was that she wished she'd brought an alarm clock.

2000: DEREK

That night he had time to himself. He'd grown used to it during the time Amy had been away. During the first time she'd been away. He was surprised how quickly it had happened, how quickly his life had reformed around her absence. He'd been a bit angry – confused and upset, of course. But despite those flickering feelings he'd found his life without her wasn't that different. Like Jell-O, his consciousness. Half-set Jell-O. It just slid right on into the holes where she used to be. It didn't push back quite as smoothly, though; didn't push smoothly out of the holes when she came back to fill them up again. Perhaps the Jell-O had gone past half set by the time she got back. These were the sort of ridiculous comparisons that filled his head when he was left to his own devices.

Mostly, now, his time was taken up with missing Benjamin. Sure, the renewed absence of Amy was duly noted – he had to remember to go to the store before the toilet paper ran out, had a lot more of the bed to himself, and of course, had to look after Paul by himself. But the real pain – the deep, persistent ache in the pit of his stomach – was for Benjamin.

In those first few weeks after Benjamin had disappeared he hadn't had much of a chance to think about it; had had a nagging sense of something missing, sure, but mostly his mind had been full with the baby, the house, work . . . And then there had been Amy. Amy not there with him at all, despite her occasional physical presence, not even once Paul had come along. If anything, she'd become even more distant after Paul's birth. By the time she vanished altogether, it had been weeks since they'd spoken. It seemed like she had just desiccated, that if he'd looked more closely he might have found the powdered residue of her left behind on the living room rug. But he didn't look too closely – just ran the vacuum cleaner over it every fortnight, like he always had. If it hadn't been for the phone number – her handwriting, he knew that at least – that had come in the mail those months later (with 'in case Paul needs it' scrawled on the back) he might have believed she'd never existed. He put the phone number inside a book of Shakespeare and mostly forgot about it.

Once Amy had left for good, his days had become almost unmanageably full. He took Paul to the hospital with him, had him stay in the hospital crèche while he worked shifts, at whatever time those shifts were. And every single day, without fail, he would look out the doors when the elevator stopped at the third floor, glance up the corridor, just in case. And when she wasn't there, which was every time, he would paste a memory of her over whatever was happening in front of his eyes, stick her to the scene like fuzzy-felt. Every day he would ask the woman at the front desk, 'Did anyone leave any messages for me?' And every day, no one had. He checked the outpatients' roster for the first three weeks, knowing that she'd be needing regular checkups to make sure her transplant was taking well but she was never there. He figured she must be seeing a doctor closer to her home, knowing he had no idea where her home was. On the bus, Paul on his lap, he'd flick his head from side to side, watching the pedestrians, staring into the windows of cars, knowing she was out there somewhere. He'd feel it, feel that she was close by and always fear that he'd been looking the wrong way at just the wrong time. He woke up every morning with a sore neck.

He wished Benjamin had had a chance to meet Paul. He felt stupid, feeling that way, what with Paul not being the flesh of his flesh, not being anything for him to feel particularly proud about. Even so, he would have liked to share his son with Benjamin. He would have liked to see her hold Paul in her lap; knew Paul would have made her smile.

Ah, whatever . . .

He kept finding himself sitting at the kitchen table, staring at the Polaroid of her in her hospital bed, the Polaroid he'd taped to the fridge door even before Amy had gone. It was fading now from the direct sunlight. He should probably put it away somewhere. He would. Tomorrow, maybe. Half an hour would pass with him sitting and staring and thinking, half an hour when he should have been warming a bottle. He was fucking useless and it was driving him crazy.

He kept writing her letters. He was desperate for conversation with her, and one-way conversation was better than nothing. The thing was, he wasn't angry with her anymore. He just wanted to let her know what a difference she'd made to his life, how she'd been there just when everything had fallen apart around him and that she'd made all of that no big deal. That these days he *felt* a lot more than he ever had, even though right now most of it was hideous, and that he was pretty pleased about that. He'd mail the letters, too; mail them to fictitious addresses. He never used her real name – it didn't sit comfortably with him and, besides, what would be the point?

So he'd write and write, stare, write some more, feed Paul, go to work, change Paul, write, stare, write. And tonight, alone again, Paul in bed, he was finishing up his latest letter.

I miss you. If I had even the foggiest idea where you

were, I'd come to your house right now and hug you and scratch behind your ears because I love you and I miss you.

For a long time before you came along, my self had huddled inside its dark meaty cell. But you got past this wall of flesh and expectations to cradle my tired brain in your safe hands. When I gave you my darkest thoughts you took them to the park, played with them, tickled their tummies and sent them back to me with smiles on their faces. Your words wrapped a warm blanket around me and your skin smelt like home. I wanted to curl up and sleep forever in the nimbus where our edges smeared.

He hoped his brain was going to get tired of this game soon, find a new rut to trudge along. Really, any old rut would do.

He folded the letter into an envelope, went into the lounge room and looked for his copy of *The Idiot* but there was a gap on the shelf between *Disgrace* and *Glamorama*. He shuffled through the papers on the kitchen counter, looked under the bed and behind the toilet but it was gone. Maybe Amy had taken it. He gave up looking, turned on the TV. He switched to the football and lay down on the couch under a blanket; lulled himself to sleep with the commentators' phrases, dreamed of them coming from between Benjamin's lips.

2022: BENJAMIN

Coming up the stairs, Benjamin noticed something stuck on her door. Aw, she thought, he left me a note. Why didn't he leave it inside? Oh god, I bet he's lost his key already.

When you wake up with the ear plugs in for the first time, it feels as though you are underwater and someone is pressing their thumbs into your ears. # 27.

Oh for Christ's sake. She peeled the note off the door, let herself in, crushed it up, and dropped it in the bin. She ran her mind back over the evening while pouring herself a glass of wine. They hadn't been that loud, surely. Well, perhaps.

Goddamn number 27. Crazy wig-wearing weirdo. Fuck him.

She put Dead Kennedys on the stereo and turned the stereo up past half. And got out her tap shoes. And started vacuuming.

Goddamn fucking 27. Sounded like he was chasing mice with a sledgehammer down there. She could hear him through the heating ducts, reading to himself, out loud, in Russian and it was making her stupid arm throb.

About half an hour later she took pity. Turning down the stereo, slipping off her tap shoes, she remembered Paul. What's happened to Paul? No messages on the answering machine, no notes on the kitchen table. No roses on the pillow. No Paul. She had a quick search around the bedroom – his stuff, his crumpled shirt and his toothbrush, seemed to be gone. That, she thought, was probably that. Never mind.

She poured another glass of wine and assessed the state of the pantry. There wasn't a whole lot going on. What I need, she thought, are the ingredients for a mind-blowing pasta. To the store!

As she stepped out onto the landing number 27 was taking his rubbish out to the dumpster. He's wearing a Harpo Marx wig. His left arm is in a sling, and has been for as long as she's known him, which is as long as she's lived upstairs from him. Twenty-two years, give or take. He's wearing a blue polyester suit; it seems to be the same blue polyester suit he's always wearing. He has the narrowest shoulders and the smallest feet.

She's spoken to him just twice. The first, just after moving in here. Their conversation went like this:

Her: 'Hi. How are you?'

Him: 'Chto?'

Her: 'HOW ARE YOU?'

Him: 'Chto?'

The second time was at the corner store, maybe two years back. He was looking at soup. He seemed, in fact, to be reordering the soup.

'You alphabetising the soup?' she asked him.

'Nyet,' he'd said, not looking at her, gripping a can of lobster bisque. 'By colour. By colour.'

He shifted cans to the left, to the right, holding two similarly red cans up to the light, squinting.

'Would you mind if I just . . .' Benjamin had reached across him to pick up a can of minestrone and he grabbed her arm.

'Please,' he'd said, 'if you could take it from . . .'

She had felt a sudden, terrible pain where his hand held her and for a second a ceiling – not the right ceiling – whirled before her. He had gripped her tighter, stared at her scar, at her face and dropped her arm.

'Later,' he muttered, 'I finish later,' and he had scuttled from the store. That night, there were no duct-side readings.

Today she ducks back behind the banister, out of his line of sight. When he rounds the corner of the corridor – those red leather boots he always wears clomping on the floorboards – she makes for the front door, quick and quiet.

The corner store had nothing that could in any way contribute to a mind-blowing pasta. She bought another bottle of red wine and a packet of macaroni cheese. Went back and bought a greenish tomato. Went back again and bought some earplugs, two mousetraps and a cookie.

'Do you have a pencil I could borrow?' she asked the man behind the counter. She said hello to him every weekday morning on her way to the bus but he still had no idea who she was.

'Here.'

He slid a pen across the counter to her while ringing up her third series of purchases.

'Um, do you have a pencil?'

'Oh. Right. Hang on.'

He handed her her third bag and on it she wrote SORRY, only it wasn't very neat.

'Thanks.'

She left the bag on her neighbour's doorstep, wishing she knew Russian for 'sorry'. She opened the new bottle of wine and poured herself a glass. The colour of the macaroni cheese powder was terrifying so she stuck the box up the back of the cupboard and made herself a tomato sandwich. Acutely aware of every noise she was making, she plugged her headphones into the stereo, lay down on the smoothed carpet and drank, upside down, listening to Pink Floyd. She didn't hear the phone ring.

The pop of the play button as the tape finished woke her up. Her neck hurt. She extricated herself from the headphones, brushed her teeth, put on her Raiders T-shirt and slid under the quilt, all without quite waking up. The pillow, she noticed, didn't smell like Paul.

And as sleep dripped out of her sinuses and into her eyes, through the heating duct she heard him. In English.

"Do you know, Totski, this is all very like what they say goes on among the Japanese?" said Ptitsin. "The offended party there, they say, marches off to his insulter and says to him, 'You insulted me, so I have come to rip myself open before your eyes'; and with these words he does actually rip his stomach open before his enemy, and considers, doubtless, that he is having all possible and necessary satisfaction and revenge. There are strange characters in the world, sir!"

And the sound of his kettle boiling and her own hand, in her sleep, reaching to wrap around a hot cup of tea.

2022: PAUL

It would have been the easiest thing in the world to stay here for the rest of my days. Easier than emigrating to Mexico, anyway, which seemed like it would be easier than trying to get my life back. Dad was, as always, flawlessly kind to me, but in an exhausting way. He asked where I was going and when I'd be back. When I drank beer in front of the television he'd raise his eyebrow at my third bottle and bring me a glass of water. But at least he didn't make me watch football for more than half an hour at a time.

The tinyness of the apartment was undeniable. And with neither of us working, and Sharrie being a fat, overgrown lump of a dog, the place was pretty much full the whole time.

Thus, the hours spent on the telephone yesterday. 'Yes, Paul Crawford. No, I don't have a permanent address, but I can . . . Yes, I was at 1733 Davenport . . . No, I don't know. They didn't tell me. Hmm, well you're not alone in that. Nothing. OK, I'll try them. Thank y–'

'Yes, that's my ID number. No. Yes. Do you want me to read it again? Yes, that's it . . . Uh huh, so I've been led to believe. Despite that, I don't feel deceased. Is it freaking you out, talking to me? Want me to give a message to your grandma? What? Oh, come on, I was just joking. No, I . . . shit.'

'Well, if you could ask him to give me a call when he does come in. He said what? No, I wasn't subletting it. God, has he no shame? Yeah, OK. Sure. Yes, I'm well aware of the tightness of the rental market. Yeah, no shi. . . sorry. Yep, well, ask him to call me, would you? Thanks.'

'Hi Benjamin, it's Paul again. So, ah, I'm probably going to be in town tomorrow, so give me a call so I can, you know, get your stuff back to you. Maybe we can go have a drink or something, or whatever. OK, later. Oh, the number. 06 3122 8476. Yep. OK, bye.'

But out of all of it, I did discover a few interesting things. I called Identity's head office to see if I could work out how I'd suddenly become altogether dead. Backtracking through their records, the woman I spoke to established that they hadn't wiped me out due to a report from Births, Deaths & Marriages, but rather that they'd come to the conclusion that my initial registration had been an error. That I'd never existed. Proclaiming me deceased was their way of tidying up.

'You know,' I told her, 'I've been hanging around

this country now for at least 22 years: going to school, getting medical attention, doing a stint at college, registering my dog, opening various bank accounts. Took you a while to work out I didn't exist, didn't it?'

'Well, sir, I –'

'Which isn't surprising,' I rudely interrupted (I'd discovered a whole new interpretation of manners during my last few days' phone calls), 'as I actually have existed – and still, as a matter of fact do exist – I've existed all this time. So really what's surprising is that you'd decide at this point that I never did. What's up with that?'

'Well, according to our database, you have no parents. That makes it hard for you to have been born, you see.'

'No parents? Hey Dad,' with my hand half over the mouthpiece, shouting to the room. I was faking here, Dad being out on another interminable walk with Sharrie. 'Dad, this woman says you don't exist either. There'll be no one left soon if they're not careful. So, miss,' turning my full attention back to the phone, 'you're saying you have no records for Derek Crawford either.'

'Oh no, not at all. We have a full record of Mr Crawford, but he's not your parent.'

'Right.'

'Sorry.'

'Oh, honestly . . . OK, what about my mother?'

'Sorry?'

'Amy Crawford, now deceased.'

'Our records don't show Ms Crawford as being deceased. Alive, no offspring.'

'Boy, you guys sure do have some fucked-up records.'

'Not really called for, is it?'

'Oh, I don't know. Under the circumstances and all.'

'I see. Is there anything else I can help you with?'

'In addition to what? This big fat pile of fuck-all?'

'It's been a pleasure, Mr Crawford.'

'Likewise.'

So I either had a bunch of questions for Identity (none of which, I suspected, they would have the appropriate records to answer) or a bunch of questions for Dad. Like, how come Benjamin never returned my calls? OK, that wasn't one of them, but still.

That night, over curry, I started in. 'Dad – if that is, in fact, your name – Identity tell me we're not related.'

'And?'

'DAD, they say you're not my dad.'

He put down his spoon, pulled his chair out a bit, sat up straighter and looked me right in the eye.

'And this is news to you?'

'What are you talking about, Dad?'

'Jesus, Paul! We're completely different colours! Of course I'm not your dad!'

'But, well, I thought it was just some weird genetic

throwback or something. Dad? You're not for real are
you?'

'God, Paul, you're serious, aren't you? Oh dear . . .
Oh, I'm sorry we didn't have this talk earlier. It's just,
well, I figured you would have worked it out yourself, what with me being black and all. Oh, Paul, I'm
sorry!'

I stared at him.

'Hehm.' He cleared his throat. 'Paul, I think you
and I need to have a little talk. You see, the thing is,
I'm not actually your dad. Don't misunderstand me,
Paulie: I love you as much, if not more so, than I
would if I were your biological father. And I think of
myself as your dad, of course I do.'

'Dad! You're laughing!'

'Oh, I'm sorry. I know, it's not funny. But I do love
you, Paulie, you know that.'

'Well, *Derek*,' and I gave him a pointed look, 'who
the hell *is* my dad?'

'Absolutely no idea.'

'What?'

'I've got no idea. None whatsoever.'

'I see. That's fab. How about my mother? Did she
know who my dad was? Is?'

'She had no idea either.'

'Great. That's great. What are you saying, Derek?
Are you calling my mother a slut? You understand
I'd have to take exception to that.'

'Absolutely. You wouldn't be her son if you didn't. If, indeed, you *are* her son.'

'Fuck off, Dad.'

'Paul! Language!'

'Sorry. Fuck off, Derek.'

'That's better.'

'So?'

'Oh, right. Well – and, really, I'm sure I've told you this before – some three years after your mother and I were married, she disappeared. Now, my under-standing was that she had, um, misunderstood her sexuality at the time of marrying me and that, in fact, she was, well, rather more interested in women than she was in men.'

'Mum was gay.'

'Well, she thought she might be. She felt she needed to find out.'

'I see. Mum left you for another woman.'

'Thanks for sparing my feelings. Yes, that's pretty much it. Haven't I told you this before?'

'Oh, I don't know, Dad, you probably have. I must have been high on crack or something. Don't look at me like that. I'm joking, you old fool. So she left you for another woman but she came back to you. What, she'd discovered she was wrong?'

'I don't think so. But she had discovered she was pregnant. And I don't think things with this woman had gone too well. So she came back. It wasn't much of a marriage after that, though.'

'Hang on. OK, let me get this straight. Mum left you for another woman, got pregnant, and came back to you to have the baby, who was me. Derek, that doesn't make a lick of sense. What, she was seeing some other guy at the time too?'

'Apparently not. Quit it with calling me Derek, would you?'

'*Dad*, that's ridiculous. You're telling me I'm the product of hot girl-on-girl sex?'

'That seems to be the only logical explanation. Amy and I didn't really talk about it much. She told me the baby wasn't mine, which was pretty damn obvious, given that sex is generally necessary for procreation, and told me there had been no other men since me. The rest, she left to my imagination. She refused to discuss it further and, quite honestly, I wasn't that interested.'

'Your wife was having another woman's child and you weren't interested?'

'Work was kind of busy at the time.'

'Oh, I see.'

He pulled his chair back in and took a few more spoonfuls. 'This is *good*, Paulie! Where'd you learn to cook like this?'

'Dad! For Christ's sake! Why didn't you tell me all this stuff before? I should be surprised I've managed to have a legal existence at all! I shouldn't even have been born!'

'Sorry, Paulie. I thought I had told you.'

'Fucking HELL, Dad!'

'PAUL!'

'Argh!'

'OK, look. There was a reason I didn't ask more questions. I was, um, rather occupied elsewhere.'

'You were seeing someone else too? Dear god, don't tell me you were experimenting too.'

'No, no, nothing like that. No, I wasn't even having an affair. I just formed, ah, rather a close friendship with a young lady who was being treated at the hospital. She'd hurt herself rather badly in a streetcar wreck and had to stay on the wards for several weeks. We were . . . close, I guess the word is close.'

'You were in love with her?'

'I suppose so. She was my soul mate I think. Probably my soul mate.'

'This is weirding me out.'

'I'm sorry, Paul.'

'Man.'

So we ate in silence for a while.

'Which reminds me.'

Nothing had actually reminded me. I'd just remembered.

'I can't believe I'm bringing this up. I'm sure I don't want to know the answer.'

'I'm not sure I want to know the question.'

'OK, the woman who told me about me having no

apparent parents also said Mum wasn't dead.'

'She might as well be.'

'What's that supposed to mean? You've always told me she was dead. You've been telling me that, like, since I was tiny. Dad? Why would you tell me that? Where's Mum? Jesus, Dad!'

'Oh, I don't know, Paulie. She left, she vanished. I have no idea where she went. No one knows where she went. Her parents never heard from her, none of her friends. The police said she was gone and that I should just deal with it. Which I did. I mean, it wasn't that hard. I missed her a bit but we hadn't, as I said, been married in any real sense for a long time. So, you know, I just forgot about her and concentrated on you.'

'Gee, thanks, Dad.'

He apparently wasn't going to reply to that. I tried again.

'OK, so Mum, who might know who my dad actually is, might actually not be dead. I could have been spending weekends with my mum all this time. Thanks, Dad!'

'Look, Paul. Theoretically, she might not be dead. But she probably is. Even if she's not, she doesn't want us to know where she is. I didn't think you'd want to know that your mum didn't want to see you or me ever again. I'm sorry. Maybe that was wrong.'

'Yeah. Maybe.'

We sat. We ate. Dad had seconds but I just didn't

feel like it. Dad got the ice cream out, and we ate ice cream. I made us both a cup of tea, and we sat down in front of the television. We did that for a few hours. I calmed down a bit. Then Dad got up off the couch and picked up his sneakers.

'Night, Paul.'

'Goodnight.'

'Don't stay up too late.'

'I won't.'

'I can't believe you thought I was your dad.'

'I can't believe you lied to me about Mum.'

'Sorry.'

'Forget it.'

'Night.'

And now, this morning, I was trying to work out what to do about all of it. I felt like I was in some crappy film noir. *He knew what he had to do. He had to find the woman who had borne him; find her and bring her to justice.* Well, not justice, maybe, but bring her to a hospital or the police or something. Bring her to someone who'd sort this all out so I could be, like, in existence again.

Why wouldn't they let my mum even be my mum? I mean, she had given birth to me, hadn't she? Surely even Identity could deal with that fact. Didn't the hospital have some sort of record of my birth?

Is 'borne' even a word? Like, as a verb? So many questions; so many questions.

The phone rang. "Lo.'

'Hello. Is Paul there please? This is his friend Benjamin.'

'It's me.'

'Oh, hi Paul.'

'I've been trying to call you for ages, Benjamin.' Oh dear, did that sound frightfully needy?

'Were you getting worried you were just a one-night stand, Paulie? Worried it didn't mean anything to me?'

'Ha ha. No, just wanted to make sure I could get your stuff back to you. I'm very responsible, you know.'

'Right.'

'So anyway, I'm going to be around later today. Gotta go deal with a whole lot of stuff – you know, try to work out exactly why my life is so totally screwed. And apparently that involves filling in forms and shit. So, um, I dunno. I could drop your stuff off at your place, if you like. Stick it through the mail slot or something.'

'The mail box is inside the front door, Paulie. It's not available to passers-by.'

'Yeah, but I've got the key.'

'Oh. Of course you do. But how would you lock up afterwards?'

'Hmm, I could, um . . .'

'We could cease this nonsense right now and go have dinner together somewhere after I finish work.'

'That'd be nice.'

'Where shall I meet you?'

'How 'bout that little cocktail bar a block down from your place?'

'Sounds dandy. I'm finishing work at 5.30. Shall I meet you about seven?'

'Certainly.'

'OK. See you then.'

'Bye. Oh, hey, Benjamin?'

'Yeah?'

'Are you really "my friend"?'

'Shut up, dick.'

'Bye.'

2022: BENJAMIN

She hadn't got one minute older since the accident. Really. Not one. And she had absolutely no idea why that was.

Was she immortal? She had no idea. Had someone painted a picture of her that was in an attic somewhere, mouldering, getting ever older in her stead? She had no idea.

She'd changed jobs regularly, but that was because people changed jobs regularly, not because anyone was getting suss about her eternally youthful appearance. And she'd been in this apartment for 22 years now, with no one turning a hair at the fact that she was still as perky and spry as she'd been on day one. Maybe they didn't care or maybe they all accepted that the cosmetic surgery industry was capable of miracles.

She had mostly stopped thinking about it. There were times when she worried. She thought about her mum and dad. She hadn't seen them since the accident and they were probably dead by now. She thought about Akiko. For years Benjamin crossed the

street several times a month to avoid her, then realised one day Akiko had at some point vanished from
the neighbourhood. She thought occasionally about
Derek, who must be pushing 50 if not 55; wondered
about her enduring taste for little sprites like Paul.
It was indecent really (though not, strictly speaking,
illegal) – she was, after all, forty-four years old. But
all in all, she just kept on keeping on, kept enjoying the way she looked; kept enjoying being able to
run around and kick stuff and catch things and generally not fall down or need hip transplants or what
have you.

All of this was meandering quietly through her
mind as she sat in front of her mirror and applied a
couple of glittering appliqués to the corner of each
eyelid, glossed her lips and put her hair in pigtails.

At the bar, Paul was sitting in front of a beer –
which, she assumed, his dad had set him up with the
cash for – and a bunch of poppies. They jarred.

'Hey, Pablito.'

'Benja. These are for you.' He thrust the flowers her
way.

'Oh, your dad bought me flowers. How sweet!'

'Ha ha.'

'Sorry. Thank you, Paul, they're beautiful.'

'Can I grab you a drink?'

'Um, cosmo thanks.'

'You're so retro. Cosmopolitan for the lady, please,'

he told the bartender. 'So how was your day? Kill any toy soldiers?'

'I buried a Marine knee-deep in rotting human flesh. Painted a little smile on his teeny face. I was pretty proud of that.'

'You do great work. I should come by some time and see it in, if you'll pardon the expression, the flesh.'

'Yes. Yes you should. Here,' she scrabbled around in her purse, pulled out a tube of lip gloss, a pencil, three apparently unpaid bills then, 'this. This'll get you in for free,' handing him a guest pass.

'Thanks.'

'Yeah, well, I know you're not exactly flush right now. Thanks for the drink.'

'Oh don't worry, you'll be paying me back. If you know what I mean. And speaking of which,' except they weren't at all, 'here's . . .' his turn to search around under his bar stool in his back pack, 'your stuff.'

He passed her a little Hello Kitty bag. She peered in: her Panthers T-shirt, her keys and a little metal tin of Chococat band aids.

'Aw. Thanks, Paulie.'

'Well, you know, thanks for looking after me. It was kind of you.'

'It was my pleasure.'

'You can stick those over your heart after I take advantage of you tonight then never call you again.'

'I'll be sure to. Can I buy you another beer?'

'Sure. Bass, thanks.'

'So how was your day?' she asked while the bar-tender poured his pint. 'Did you fill in some forms?'

'Why yes, I did.'

'So what's going on?'

'OK, so it turns out the problem is that Identity was doing one of their spot-checks for terrorists, and they discovered an aberration in the records. About me. That is, they don't have any record of me having parents. They've got me, and they've got my apparent parents, but they've got nothing relating us one to the other. As a result, they've decided I don't exist. They've expunged me. Because I don't make sense and I'm messing with the spreadsheets or something.'

'Hmm. What are you going to do?'

'Well, the problem is that no one's really sure who my parents are. My dear dad, you see, isn't really my dad, he just brought me up. And my mum, who's probably dead but maybe not, but either way no one knows where she is, didn't know who my dad was.'

'Ah.'

'She's not a slut, though, you understand.'

'Of course. She's your mother. The two are mutually incompatible.'

'Exactly.'

They both drank. She drained her glass and ordered another.

'So, today I went to the hospital where I was born,' Paul went on, 'to see if they could help me out.'

'You were born here?'

'Uh huh.'

'You don't see that much these days. Most everyone's come here from somewhere else.'

'Yeah, I was born here, down at City. My dad used to work there, too, when I was a kid, which I was hoping might pull a little weight as far as access to their databases but turns out I was wrong.'

'When were you born, if you don't mind me asking?'

'June 6 2000.'

'Humph.' Surely not. Surely.

'What?'

'Huh? Oh, so you're a Gemini, then?'

'Yup. You care?'

'Not really. So, tell me what happened at the hospital.'

'Well, long story short and all, it turns out Identity are right. The hospital has no record of my birth. So for all I know I could be a fucking Virgo or something, because really I only have my dad's word – and, remember, he's not even my real dad – that I was born there, that I was born on that date. So, you see, I'm at a bit of a loss. Hit a bit of a dead end, you might say.'

'Shit, eh.'

'Absolutely.'

'So, your dad worked at the hospital when you were born, right?'

'Yeah. Not in maternity, though. He was in oncology. Which, I gather, was depressing as hell, what
with people dying just as you got close to them, then
new people coming in, who you'd inevitably get
close to, all of whom would then up and die on you.
Something of a disheartening cycle you might say,
which is why when I was three he ditched nursing and
went into health admin.'

'Your dad was a nurse?'

'Yeah. But he's not a pussy, right?'

'Sure.'

Not possible. Not possible, she thought. Too much
of a coincidence.

What the hell was he talking about now? Was he
talking about tennis? Why was he talking about
tennis? She smiled but her smiles were about the way
his mouth moved; she had no idea whether what he
was saying was amusing or not. That stubble, she
thought. Do you know you've got stubble? He was
beautiful in his obtuseness, his complete absence of
awareness of himself, right then. The stubble let her
see the outlines of his gums, teeth; the bones that held
his face together. It's like dusting for fingerprints, she
thought, the evidence of your genetic structure given
away by those tiny, negligent hairs. God, I want to
climb inside your mouth.

'Do you want to come home with me?' she said, out
loud this time.

'Um, didn't you want dinner? I . . . sure. Yes.'

'Thanks!' to the bartender. She was grabbing coat, purse, wrapping herself up against the night. Home. Now. Home and this boy, now.

Opening the two front doors, she reached for his hand.

'Gotta be quiet, OK? The guy downstairs has been a bit sensitive about noise lately.'

'Sure. As a mouse.'

Up the stairs, in the door and 'Sorry about the mess.' Slightly muffled because she was pulling off her T-shirt.

'Um.'

'Oh, I'm sorry.' Putting it back on. 'Can I get you a drink?'

'Come here.'

This, more than anything, made her feel like a girl – the sensation of being wrapped in arms twice the size of her own, held against a chest flat, broad, feeling so damn safe. It was faintly irritating, the visceral instinctiveness of it all, but good. Good.

His forehead resting against hers – was he bending down? She didn't know, lost in the closeness of it, letting go of the pain – he, talking soft and low to her, his fingers running over the stars stuck to her cheeks, peeling them off, holding them between his fingertips, whispering to her. She felt tiny.

His thumb running along the line of her jawbone,

fingers cupped behind her ear, his lips warm at the corners of her mouth, still talking, still talking; his thumb stroking her bottom lip, her bottom lip between his lips, between his teeth, her eyes still open, watching the green of his eyes blur and close, watching him for one more second, letting him be lost first, then closing her eyes too. All of herself, for now, focused on her mouth.

'OK,' he pulled away a little, close enough, still, for her to be wrapped entirely in him, close enough that the words were more breath than sound, 'now you can take it off.'

And his hands around her waist, thumbs in front, fingers behind, almost closed around her, hands sliding up across her skin, stripping away her T-shirt, stripping away everything outside of now, thumbs skirting the edges of her nipples as the T-shirt came up over her head and she saw, fleetingly, her dad helping her undress forty years ago, and pushed the thought away.

One hand back around her waist and the fingertips of the other tracing her tattoo. 'What is it?'

'*Hydrosaurus pustulatus*; Philippine sailfin.'

'It has goat eyes.'

'Yes it does. Will you please kiss me again?' and thought – thank god you didn't tuck your shirt in. So much better when you don't have to untuck a shirt, so awkward – and stroked the line between skin and belt, felt his back dip in to his spine.

'You look pretty in your bra,' was mostly lost as he was talking into her throat, hand under her jawbone again, mouth at its crux – the point where it turned up towards her ear. 'Does it match your underpants?'

'Of course it does. Take it off.'

So he took it off. Fingers, this time, pausing over her nipples.

'Beautiful girl. Do you want this off?' His hands moving to his own shirt.

'Please,' watching his abdominal muscles tighten, rib cage rise as his arms moved up over his head. 'You have flat clavicles.'

He smiled, dropped the shirt and pushed her hair behind her ear as he bent to kiss her. He ran both hands down the length of her torso, recorded the shape of her.

'Here now,' kneeling before her, unzipping her skirt and sliding it from her, kissing her belly button, stroking the line of her hip bones, kissing the line of her hip bones. 'Yes, yes they do,' sliding her underpants off as well, the hem of them catching on her boot's zipper, then unhooked and off.

'Sit down.'

On the couch, bending her knees up, foot resting on his lap down there on the floor. 'Gorgeous,' kissing her knees, small kisses, and unzipping one boot, pulling it off. 'Oh my,' distracted from the other boot, hands high on her thighs, thumbs in, his grip tight as he pulled her legs a little wider, hands higher and higher. She shifted her booted foot to his shoulder.

'I wish I was naked.'

'You could be.'

'I don't want to move from here.'

'I'm not going anywhere.'

While he stood and pulled off his jeans then under-pants, she unzipped her remaining boot. 'I see you're not having any problems with the beer today.'

'None whatsoever. Thanks for the reminder. Now, where were we?' as he knelt back down.

'I'm glad you're naked. You look lovely.' He did. Snake-hipped lovely.

'Not as lovely as this. C'mere.' She always felt a little like the subject of that painting – the one where the black-clad students watch as Dr Gray slices open the naked cadaver on a slab – in this situation. There, bent backward, his hands on her breasts, face buried between her thighs. Splayed. Warmer than the corpse, though; much warmer.

He paused and she slid off the couch and into his lap.

'Thanks.'

'Ouch. My legs don't bend that way.'

She squirmed and he unbent himself and sat back on his hands. She wiped his mouth and kissed him, legs around his waist, sitting between his thighs, right hand stroking his cock, left hand, as always, not doing much of anything.

'Do you . . .?'

'Hang on.' He stretched out towards his backpack dropped by the couch and rustled around in the dim light from the window. 'No, don't stop. I can reach without getting up.'

'Will you . . .?' passing her the condom.

He flipped her over and, as he sank into her, she gave in. Flicked the switch, dropped the curtain, released the hounds, let it all flood back over her. Let it all out. Because, really, there's nowhere more private than the floor of your living room, no lights, so close to the person inside you that they don't have a hope of seeing your expression, far too wrapped up in themself to ask where you've gone.

And later, while she slept, these were the dreams she had.

A bathroom, she knew this one, felt like she'd been there before. Lying on her back staring at the ceiling, wondering if anyone was ever going to change the bulb in that broken downlight. And then not thinking anything else.

The dream again from the first night she'd slept here: she recognised and remembered it now. Derek, in a suit, looking beautiful. A grey suit. Her hands, sort of but different, reaching out towards him and him, talking, not talking to her but about her.

Drinking whiskey and looking at rooftops from a window. Sitting in the window frame and wondering how long it would take to hit the ground. Thinking about dropping the bottle, randomly killing a passer-by. Thinking about dropping a fork, a penny, the television, a baby.

Dreaming in Russian.

2022: PAUL

It hadn't been exactly as I told her.

Yesterday the fog rolled in off the park. By two, when I hit the western neighbourhoods, the air was distinctly chill and damp, the sun doing that thing where you can stare straight at it, looking like a rayograph of itself wrapped in its cloud shroud.

And so, with the grey and the chill and the preternatural hush of echoes dampened by fog, the hospital looked to be more skulking on the hill than sitting there emotionally neutral, the way inanimate objects are supposed to. I skirted round the emergency entrance (I had had an abiding fear, since small, and with no apparent reason, that one day I would be knocked down and killed by an ambulance) and headed for the big double doors of the administration building. Behind the doors, a stale wall of hot air.

I sat on one of the waiting room's dusty pink couches, watched the woman at the desk explain to a frustrated old man that it was not possible for him to visit his wife right now, that visiting hours were over for the day, that she understood he'd come a long way but that the rules existed for a reason. She looked tired. He looked tired. I felt like lying down on the couch; felt like putting my feet up, sleeping, giving up on all of this. I flicked through the magazines.

'Sir, you can't wait there.'

He'd taken up residence on one of the couches, spread out some sandwich makings and taken off his coat. He pointed up at the sign.

She didn't have the energy to argue.

I put down the magazine and walked over.

'Hi.'

'Hello. How can I help you?'

The desk looked like it had been there since the 19th century, its dark wood totally out of place in the equally dated salmon-and-slate colour scheme.

'Hi. Um, this is kind of complicated.'

'Well, sir, if you'll give me a summary, I'll see if I can help you. If I can't, I should be able to find someone who can.'

'OK. I'm trying to get hold of a record of my birth. I was born here, in this hospital, in 2000.'

'Alright, sir. Well, you understand that birth records are kept centrally at Identity?' She was turning the ring in her ear: round, round, round.

'I know that. But they say they don't have that particular one. So I was wondering if maybe you kept copies here, copies of birth certificates of babies born in your hospital.'

'They don't have your record?'

'No, ma'am, they say they don't.'

'OK.' She reached across to the other side of the huge desk, pulled a pen from out of the cup sitting there and tested it. Scratchy. She threw it in the bin, pulled out another. 'What's your name?'

'Paul Joshua Crawford.'

'How do you spell that?'

'C.R.A.W.F.O.R.D.'

'Date of birth?'

'June 6 2000.'

'And born here, right?'

'Yup.'

'Mother's name?'

'Amy Crawford.'

'Father?'

'I don't know, sorry.'

'That's OK. We can get by without it. Identity number?'

'I could give it to you, but it doesn't work anymore.'

'I'm sorry?'

'I don't exist anymore. That's why I have to get hold of my birth certificate: Identity has taken into their collective head that I don't really exist.'

'OK. We'll make do without that then.'

She wrote some brief notes on the piece of paper, recapped the pen and put it back in the cup. 'Alright, if you can just take a seat, I'll be back in a minute.'

'Thanks,' I squinted at her name tag, couldn't make it out. 'Thanks.'

'Won't be long, Paul.'

I was seeing a lot of daytime television these days, more than I had since I was four. It's a truism, I know, but daytime TV really is very bad. I picked up a magazine. Bad. Slumped on the couch, let my head drop back, closed my eyes. Listened to the old man eat his sandwiches and talk to *Divorce Court*. He chewed loudly.

'Hey, mister, why don't you show her a little more respect. Be a little bit kind. You used to love her. Remember when you used to love her? Don't you think this hurts her too? I know you're angry, but sometimes you just have to feel the pain. Feel it.'

Chewing again.

'Mr Crawford?'

God, I was tired.

'Mr Crawford,' as I straightened the creases out of my shirt and made my way to the desk, 'I've done a simple search of the database and there isn't any record of your name. I checked admissions for the date of your birth, and no one by your mother's name was admitted that day or the day before. However, a search for your mother's name found that on,' she looked down at the print outs she'd placed on the desk, just out of my line of sight, 'June 10th of that year, a Ms Amy Crawford checked out of the hospital.

Which is odd, as we have no record of her checking in, and no record of what she was being treated for. It's possible it's an error.'

For a moment, just a moment, I rested my elbows on the desk, my head in my hands.

'Are you alright, Mr Crawford?'

'Yeah. I just, oh, I just don't know where to go from here. I never thought I'd say this, but I'd rather be at work than trying to sort this out.'

'One other thing. The search on your name pulled up a Derek Crawford, working as a nurse during that time period. Is he any relation?'

'Yeah, that's my dad. Well, he's not really my dad. My mum's husband. He was working here when I was born, working in oncology. I think he left about three years later.'

'That's right. He was let go in March 2002. March 22.'

'Sorry?'

She read from the print out: 'Derek Crawford, registered nurse, pensioned off on March 22 2002. Disability pension, it says.'

'Oh.'

'So, Paul, I don't know what else to tell you. That's what we have.'

'That's fine. That's actually quite helpful. You've been very helpful.'

'It's my pleasure. Do you want a copy of these?' Waving the print outs at me.

'Thanks, that'd be great.'

She opened a drawer in the desk, pulled out a big yellow envelope, slid the print outs into it and passed it across to me.

'There you are. You have a nice day now.'

'You too.'

I turned and walked back out through the big double doors. The fog had thickened and lowered, the wind picked up. It was cold. I had no idea where I was going. I turned right back around.

'Excuse me, miss,' as I came back in through the big double doors. 'Do you mind if I just sit here for a while?'

'You go ahead, sweetheart. Take your time.'

As I collapsed back onto the couch, the old man poked a corned beef sandwich my way. 'Want one?'

'You know, I'd love one. Thanks.'

We watched *Divorce Court* together, then reruns of *Santa Barbara*. It turned out he'd been a big fan of Robyn Wright, in her heyday. We talked about her movie work, showed each other interesting articles from the magazines and shared another corned beef sandwich. It was good.

At four o'clock, I figured I should get back on that horse. I wished the man well, waved goodbye to the woman at the desk and went back through the doors. I knew I should call Dad but my phone battery was dead. I didn't want to stand in a bus stop using a public phone: it was damn, damn cold by this time and the sun was starting to go down.

Fuck it, I thought. She won't mind. If she even found out, which I hoped she wouldn't.

I read my book till the bus came, though it was hard to follow the plot. I kept reading the same line over and over. There was no one else at the stop so I had to keep looking up to make sure the bus wasn't passing me by while I was otherwise engaged. When it came it was almost empty. There was a guy up front writing notes in the margin of a book on content management. I felt sorry for him and knew he should really be feeling sorry for me. Why wasn't he at work? He looked eminently employable; employed, even. Smooth faced and slick, groomed press-ready glossy, the only hint that he was something other than a cyborg was the red razor rash blossoming on the skin just below his ear. As he sat, thinking, reading, hopefully actually thinking about screwing rather than content management, he twisted the pen round between his fingers. The tendons of his forearms squirmed under his skin, wriggling like nervous lemmings in a microfibre sock. He had nice shoes. I thought about asking him where he'd got them, considered getting up from my seat, sitting down next to him, the only other person in the bus and striking up a conversation with him.

'Hey pal,' I'd say, 'nice shoes. Where'd you get 'em?'

And he'd say, 'Why, my mother gave them to me.

I've had to resole them twice, but look at how well the uppers are holding up.'

'They're classy,' I'd say. And then I'd ask him about the content management book and he'd admit that he didn't have a job either, that he was just trying to bone up on the business, trying to get a foot in the door as it was, at which point I'd note that with such classy footwear he was certainly one step ahead of the pack, and we'd both laugh. So I'd ask him what he read when he wasn't boning up and it would turn out that we had quite a few favourite authors in common, plus one or two on which we vehemently disagreed, and my stop would come up and I'd think, screw it. Screw this whole private eye business. I'm sick of it, sick of dealing with it. I want to go get drunk. Damn the consequences, damn them to hell, I'd think. Somewhat Errol Flynnish, Clark Gableish, I was, in this sequence.

'My name's Paul,' I'd say. 'Want to go get a beer?' 'You're darn tootin,' he'd reply and, thus, we would. It'd be great. It'd be loads of fun.

Three more weeks of unemployment, three more weeks of not existing, I was guessing, and I'd actually start doing stuff like that. But I couldn't help saying, over my shoulder, as I went out the door, 'nice shoes.'

'Hey, thanks!' he said. 'Want to go get a beer?' As the door closed behind me.

The stop was four blocks up the hill from Benjamin's

place. I grabbed a bunch of flowers from the corner store on my way down. I'd give them to her at the bar; with luck I wouldn't have to mention why I'd felt it morally necessary to buy them. I pulled the keys out of the Hello Kitty bag I'd dropped them in earlier that day and let myself in through the two front doors.

Her place was looking pretty normal, thankfully. I'd been a bit worried that there might have been underpants strewn around or someone sleeping in the bed or evidence of Satan worship or something, something I'd have trouble not mentioning later in the night. But it was all fine, pretty much as I'd left it the other morning. I sat down on the couch and pulled the phone towards me.

Four rings, and the answering machine clicked in. 'You've called Derek. I'm not here right now [barking in the background]. Leave a message and I'll call you back.'

'Hey Dad, this is Paul. I'm not anywhere you can reach me right now. It's, um,' I leaned forward to decipher the microwave clock, a good ten feet away, '4.50. I'll give you a call back later this afternoon.'

Benjamin had said she'd be finishing work at around 5.30. I figured I'd call him back in ten minutes and if he wasn't there, I'd go find a café with a public phone and call him from there later on. Till then, I'd rummage through her bathroom cabinet and see if I could get any dirt on her. Or not.

Instead, I napped. I'd perfected the six-minute nap, the one where you lie down right on the edge of the couch. The theory being that as you hit REM sleep, your leg – without fail – will twitch, and you'll fall on the floor. It's a refreshing break without the terminal retardation that 20 minutes' deep sleep can bring on.

5.04 by the microwave clock. I called back as promised.

'Derek Crawford speaking.'

'Dad, it's me.'

'Hey, Paulie. How are you? I was just in the bathroom when you called. Sorry I didn't get to see you before you left this morning. Sharrie was really enjoying her walk.'

'Of course she was.'

'Are you alright? Recovered alright from last night's various minor traumas? Should I be sending you for professional help?'

'I'm fine, Dad.'

'How did it go today? Any good news?'

'Dad, what the hell is up with you? Can you not stop talking for a second?'

'_'

'Thank you. So, Dad, they tell me at the hospital that you were actually fired.'

'They're allowed to tell you stuff like that? Isn't that private?'

'Well, I don't know. But they told me.'

'I wasn't fired. I was let go.'

'Same diff.'

'Not really.'

'So why did you tell me you quit?'

'Because you were, like, 12 when you asked me why I'd stopped nursing. As if I was going to tell you I'd been fired. Let go. I'm surprised you even remember me telling you anything.'

'Kids remember shit, Dad. It was important to me. I liked that you'd worked at the hospital where I'd been born. It made me feel safe. Like if something bad happened to me, I could just hang around with you, same as always. I wouldn't have to go to some weird place, with strangers. Because you'd know what to do. I guess it's sort of like those kids feel whose parents work in the cafeteria. Every day it's like there's a little bit of home with you.'

'I see.'

He clearly wasn't going to elaborate. 'So what's the story?' I asked.

'Does it really matter now?'

'Well, kind of. You know, while we're finding stuff out, telling a few dark secrets. Now seems like the perfect time.'

'Hmm.'

'Spill.'

'I can't believe I brought you up to be such a rude young man.'

'Dad . . .'

'Alright. So, you were two, almost three years old. It'd been pretty much just you and me for quite a while. Amy had spent less and less time with us those first months after you were born and, eventually, 'round November of 2000, she just vanished. I didn't realise for quite a while – like I said, she'd been gone more and more, it wasn't that unusual for her to be out of the house a few days at a time. But when she didn't show after ten days, I called her parents, called the couple of friends who were still talking to me. No one had heard from her. Eventually we filed a missing person report with the police, after she'd been gone a couple of weeks. As far as I know, nothing ever came of it – they've certainly never bothered to call me. I fell out of touch with her parents, who'd never liked me much anyway. Don't know if it was the black thing, or the foreign thing, or just that Amy didn't like me much either, but anyway. A few years later, I got a call from someone claiming to be Amy.'

'Mum called you?'

'She said she wanted to see me, wanted to see you. I asked her where she'd been, why she'd waited so long to get in touch but she said she'd rather not talk about it. So we organised to meet up. Mostly we talked about you. I explained potty training – do you want to hear about that now?'

'Not right now, thanks. I'd rather get to the bit where you get canned from work.'

'It's coming. I told her how many nappies you got through in a day, outlined your sleeping patterns, described the crèche at work, all that sort of thing. And, eventually, after three glasses of wine, she blurted it out. "Derek," she said, "I want Paul to come and live with me." I was furious. Do you want to hear what I yelled at her? I made rather a scene in that restaurant, not at all typical for me.'

'I can imagine, Dad. You can skip the details if you like.'

'So, I made it clear that there was no way on earth that would be happening. I'd been taking such damn good care of you for the last two years with barely a word of thanks from her, no help from her parents, nothing. "Derek," she said, "yell all you like. He's my child. You're not even related to him. You don't have a hope in hell of keeping him." Or words to that effect. Basically, she threatened to take me to court. You were my whole life, Paul. I couldn't have lived without you.' Derek cleared his throat. 'Excuse me. Sorry.' There was another pause, and he continued. 'Well, I asked a lawyer what my chances were like and she pretty much concurred with Amy's opinion that my chances were less than those of a snowball in hell. I couldn't take it, Paul, couldn't take the stress and the fear, the fear of losing you. I mean it, Paul. At that time, I really would have had absolutely nothing without you. Nothing. The subpoena came in and I cracked, cracked under the strain of it all. I still had to work, had to pay for your food and your nappies, had to make sure I was still a good father, make sure the court knew I was a good father but it was getting harder and harder to do my job properly. I lost some things. Stole some things. I had some terrible visits to your mother; just terrible. And one day I mixed up dosages, we almost lost a patient. She didn't die but it was close. And I knew things were about to come crashing down. So, I . . . Sharrie! Drop that! Hang on, Paul.'

He dropped the receiver, and I could hear him admonishing the dog. I didn't believe for a second that Sharrie was even in the room.

'Where was I? Oh yeah, I was fired.'

'Dad, what were you really going to say? Obviously there's more to it. You didn't lose me.'

'Paul, I falsified the hospital records. I diddled the computer system and removed the record of your mother's admission, removed the record of your birth. I didn't know what else to do. I didn't want to lose you.'

'You forgot to remove the bit about her being discharged, Dad. They've still got that.'

'Really? My. Oh dear.'

'I guess that's a fairly major crime. To say nothing of the fact that it's totally fucked up my life.'

'I know, I know. God. I'm sorry. It just seemed like the right thing to do. You wouldn't have been happy with your mother.'

'Well, thanks for making that decision for me.'

'Oh, Paul, you were only two. How could you have known what was best for you?'

'Well, I dunno. At least I was *sane*.'

'_'

'So it worked, then?'

'Case was thrown out. Amy had no way of proving you were her child, and as she was obviously pretty unstable anyway, they assumed she was just some lunatic.'

'Poor Mum. God, Dad, how could you do that to her?'

He didn't answer.

'But they fired you anyway?'

'Yes – yes they did. The heartless bastards.'

'Well, aren't you full of surprises. I guess this is why I usually go months without calling you.' I'd had enough of this conversation. I needed some space to think. 'Dad, I've gotta go. I'm going to meet Bennie for dinner, give her back her things. See you later, OK?'

Oh, god, I would so have liked to lie back on the couch and sleep. Sleep, or cry, or laugh hysterically. But it was 5.36 and Benjamin was due home from work any minute. While there was a good chance she'd understand what the hell I was doing crying on her couch once I explained myself, I didn't want to deal with the expression on her face when she first came through that door and didn't want to deal with repeating everything I'd just heard. I lay there for a minute, listening to the aeroplanes flying overhead, thinking about maybe grabbing a cab to the airport and heading for Peru. I wondered if my passport worked anymore, wondered where my mummy was. In the end I did what one always does in times of unbearable internal conflict: I went for a beer.

And the rest, as they say, is history.

—

I woke up the next morning to someone talking right into my ear.

'Paul?'

The voice sounded vaguely familiar.

'Paul, I'm hungry.'

I opened one eye and confirmed that it was Benjamin.

'Paul, do you want to come have some breakfast with me?'

'Mmm. You're not going to work?'

'It's Saturday, Paul.'

'Don't I have to go fight City Hall today?'

'It's Saturday, Paul. City Hall is lining up for breakfast.'

I rolled over and patted my hair back into place. 'Oh. OK, let's go meet them then. They owe me a cup of coffee.'

'Yes. Yes they do. I'm going to have a shower. Here – watch this and tell me what happens.'

She flicked the remote, turned on a football game.

I went back to sleep.

When I woke up she was clean and damp and I was awake because she was smacking my head.

'Paul! You're supposed to be watching!'

'I can't stand that crap. Don't make me.' She looked nice. No T-shirt today; instead she had on a tight-fitting button-up shirt, casually somewhat unbuttoned. I could see the top of the lizard climbing out from her cleavage. 'Don't think you can convert me by pointing out the beauty of the game. Don't think I'm going to be thrilled by any comparisons with chess or warfare, neither of which I give a damn about either. I've heard it all a thousand times from my dad, and none of it, ever, has made even the tiniest bit of difference to me.'

'I'm starting to think I should be dating your dad instead.'

'Well, maybe you should. Do you want me to set you up?'

'Ah, I reckon he's probably a bit old for me.'

'Well, sure but he's pretty well preserved what with the 500 mile walks he takes the damn dog for every day.'

'Well, I'll keep it in mind. Perhaps when I'm tired of your gorgeous, hard young body I'll give him a call.'

'What, this old thing?' I pulled the sheet down to show off my pecs which, incidentally, I had been putting a little work into during my period of unemployment. You know, lifting soup cans and the like.

'Yeah, that's the one.'

'You're supposed to be overcome by lust.'

'Oh I am, I am. It's just my blood sugar's getting really low and I'm worried I'll pass out during the heat of passion.'

'That's alright. As long as you lie still that won't be a problem for me. You don't swallow your tongue or anything icky, do you?'

She was staring at my hand, wrapped around hers. I waited for her to yell at me for being gross but she just kept staring.

'You OK there?' I asked.

'What? Oh.' She looked up at me and reassembled a smile. 'Go have a shower, will you, so we can go eat?'

When I got out of the shower the TV was off.

'What's up?'

'Oh, they lost. Can't fight fate, I guess. Food?'

'Certainly.'

'Grab the spare key, just in case. It's where you dropped it.'

So later, drinking coffee, her reading the sports news on her phone, me looking at the list of people who've unfriended me, waiting for our food, and she suddenly lifts her head and says, 'I'm having the most awesome déjà vu.'

'Still?'

She looked at a point somewhere past my shoulder for a moment. 'Talking wrecked it. But it was; it was a total, full on déjà vu.'

'You've probably been here before. You know, eating breakfast. What with it being two blocks from your house.'

'I know, I know, but that was different. That feeling. It was like I'd been here before, but not as me. As someone different. Oh!'

An 'ah, of course, silly me' kind of 'oh!' it was. She picked up her phone again.

'What? You can't "Oh!" like that then go back to the sports news. What?'

'Honestly, it won't make any sense to you.'

'What?'

'It's sort of a private in-joke, but just with me.'

'Right. Tell me.'

'It was my arm. My arm's been here before.'

'Yes. Yes you probably brought it with you one time when you came for breakfast. To, you know, help with lifting food to your mouth and stuff.'

'No, the other arm. The arm that didn't used to be mine. My arm transplant,' and she waved her left arm at me. 'See, I told you it wouldn't make any sense to you.'

Arm transplant? That was a transplant? Wow, she had someone else's arm. Cool!

'Hang on. You're saying you feel things that your arm did when it was someone else's arm?'

'That's right.'

'Sort of like how people feel their own limb, phantom limb, after they've had an amputation, only in reverse?'

'Not really, no. That's a really lame attempt at an explanation, Paul.'

'Sorry. That's all I know about amputees. Hey, I'm screwing an amputee! Cool! Did you know James Dean was way into that?'

'Paul, you're an insensitive bastard.'

'I know. Sorry. Please, tell me more about the psychic messages you receive from your transplanted arm.'

'I will not.'

'Oh, go on. Really. I mean it. Sorry for teasing you.'

'Fuck you.'

'Pleeeeeeeeeeeeeease. I've never known anyone who heard stories from their arm before. Go on.'

'OK. It was like this.' She narrowed her eyes and looked into the middle distance.

. . . in a café, watching a woman over her breakfast, trying to concentrate on the conversation, thoughts louder than the words . . . I want to breastfeed you like a baby, to hold your fragile newborn head, to know you as you were

when you were fresh and wondering and alive.

She blushed a little, acted as though she was adding more sugar to her coffee as she asked me, 'Does it make any sense to you? It doesn't make any sense to me. I guess she was here, with someone, like this, whoever she was. She looked a bit like you, the woman she was watching. But perhaps that was just the overlay of you sitting there. Like in a medical dictionary – the sheets that make up the layers of the body.'

'Strangely, I know exactly what you mean. About the dictionary. No idea about the other stuff, though.'

'It hasn't happened to me for ages. When I first got this arm it used to tell me stories all the time. I guess as it became more a part of my body, assimilated, it forgot some of its history. I think it still sends me dreams sometimes. I have weird dreams.'

'Poached eggs?'

I smiled at the waitress, wondered if she'd heard what Benjamin was saying. 'They're mine. Thanks.'

'So this special must be yours, right?'

'That's right. Thanks.'

'Enjoy your meals.'

I suddenly remembered a dream I'd had. 'I dreamed someone was saying my name last night.' I just as suddenly realised what a boring dream it was. 'It was probably you, I guess.'

'I doubt it,' she was smiling through a mouthful of eggs. 'The guy downstairs talks into my heating duct sometimes. Maybe it was him.'

'Sorry?'

'My downstairs neighbour. He talks into my heating duct for hours on end.'

'Doesn't that freak you out?'

'He's been doing it for years – I'm pretty used to it. Mostly he just reads to me in Russian.'

'OK, that's weird.'

'English too. I think it's Tolstoy or one of those old Russian guys he's reading. Sometimes I recognise bits and pieces but I think that's cause he reads the same stuff over and over.'

'That's definitely weird.'

'I'm sure he's not really reading to me. I think he just likes the spot by the duct – it's warm there. And sound travels up through the ducts as you may have noticed. That'd be cool if he'd taken a fancy to you though. That'd get him off my back.'

'Benjamin, I don't think your downstairs neighbour knows my name.'

'Oh, he probably does. He likes to see a CV of anyone I bring home with me. You know, just to make sure I'm spending time with quality. He cares.'

'I believed you for a second.'

She kissed me then. Which was nice. Except I got egg on my face.

'What are you going to do with your day today, Pablito?'

'I don't know. You know, it's been go, go, go the

last few days and still nothing resolved. All this time I've been wishing I didn't have to do any of it but now that I don't have to do any of it I don't know what to do. I guess cause I still haven't resolved any of it. You know? I should be looking for somewhere to live but there's probably no point because I don't have any income, do I, or any credit record or any ID number. All of which tends to be required.'

'The offer to stay at my place still stands,' she said. 'You can stay over the weekend, at least, if you like. Give your dad a break.'

Give me a break from Dad more like, I thought. But I said, 'I'd really like that, actually. That'd be really kind.'

'OK then.'

'So what are you doing today?'

'I've got to go into work for a bit. There's some things I have to wrap up.'

'You're building ancient Egyptian dioramas?'

'Sorry? Oh, right. Lame.'

'Well, in that case I might just go back to your place and grab my book and go read in the park for a while.'

'Sounds divine.' She wiped the last of the egg off her cheek and pushed her chair out from the table.

'Shall I make you some dinner?' I needed to pay her back somehow.

'Oh, yes please. That'd be great,' as I got up too and followed her to the door. 'I'll grab wine. Red or white?'

'Red, I'm thinking. Oh, do you eat meat?'

'Sure do.'

'Of course you do, you red-blooded, football-watching woman, you.'

'That's me. See you tonight then, chicken liver.'

And another kiss. This is turning into a regular, like, relationship. I watched her standing outside till the bus came then headed back up the hill.

When I got back the sun was sitting square on the bottom twelve steps of the staircase. It was an offer too good to refuse. Parks, after all, are windy and full of homicidal cats. I went upstairs and made myself a cup of tea. I grabbed a pillow off the bed, pulled my book from my backpack and took a handful of cookies from the pantry.

Warm sun, squishy pillow, toffee and pecan cookies. Consoling myself with Kafka. Knowing exactly how he felt.

And wondering, when is it polite to ask about the arm? I mean, I wouldn't have known that her arm was a transplant if she hadn't mentioned it today. I figured it was just, you know, not fully functional. But, shit, it's someone else's arm. I'd really like to know more about that, about what that feels like. But I don't know if I can ask. Don't know if I can even ask how it happened, what sort of accident it was. I guess it was some childhood thing, so maybe it's no big deal now. Or maybe I should just wait till she tells me of her own accord. Dad would know; maybe I should ask Dad. I'll call him later.

The guy with the wig came through the front door. Was this the guy Benjamin was talking about? The crazy Russian guy? He certainly looked crazy. Crazy and small. I got up off the pillow and made to move out of the way.

'Please, do not be moving on my account. I have almost no desire to go upstairs to my small, dark apartment so your stopping me is of no great consequence.'

That'd be him.

As he passed me he looked up for a moment, stared at my face and I felt suddenly, deeply and profoundly that this man was my mother. My hand reached out – I don't remember telling it to reach out – to touch his shoulder and I was swept with relief as he pushed by without noticing. My mother! What was I thinking?

But then he turned again to look over his shoulder at me and I was sure. I was sure. Why else would he be looking at me like that? Why else other than that I am his son.

'Mum?'

'*Chto*?'

'Mum?' God, what was I saying. 'Is it you, Mum? Mum, if it's you, you have to tell me. It's me, Paul. I can't – look, my life is all messed up and I can't fix it until I find you and I've found you, so –'

Shit.

'I don't know what you are talking about.' He turned his back to me and started taking the stairs two at a time. I leapt after him.

'Wait! Wait, just a moment. Look, just come and have a cup of tea. Just some tea. We'll chat! Reminisce! Please.' I grabbed his arm and forced him – I don't want to say 'forced', but let's be honest that's what it was – up the corridor to Benjamin's apartment. 'It's just in here. Just here. Come on, I'll make you some tea and we can talk.' He sighed and dug his heels in but he seemed to have given up the fight so I wrestled the door open and shoved him through. Then I deadlocked the door behind us and put the key in my pocket.

'Right,' I said. 'Where were we? Tea? Oh, fuck.' And then I fell on the couch and prayed this would all go away really, really soon.

—

I sit here on the couch in the apartment of a woman I barely know and look across at the narrow messy bed where a rumpled middle-aged man is lying on his back, smoking a cigarette. I try to stop my brain trickling out my ears.

The man rolls over on one elbow and squints at me through his cigarette smoke. I need to explain myself and let him go home but I don't even know where to start. Maybe with letting him go home. I stand up to unlock the door and he stubs out his cigarette and says to me, 'Are you Paul?'

His accent is gone and his hair is sliding off the pillow and on to the floor.

I nod and unlock the deadbolt.

He rolls onto his back again, pushes his hand into his slacks pocket and pulls out a cigarette packet. 'You want a smoke, Paul?'

I shake my head. 'No thanks. I'm sorry. If you want to go home –' I wave lamely at the door.

He isn't getting up. Instead, he's lighting another cigarette.

'Where were you born, Paul?' he asks me.

'Here,' I say, still feebly hanging on to the door handle. 'At City.'

'On?'

'On?' I repeat, not understanding what he's asking of me.

'On which day were you born here, at City?'

'Oh. June 6 2000.'

He lies there on his back and smokes and stares at the ceiling for a while and I wonder if I should just sit down again. Perhaps I could walk out the door and never come back, leaving Benjamin to deal with whatever mess this is I've cooked up now.

'I'm sorry I made you come here,' I manage to say.

'I've been unwell,' and I realise I have; that I have become unwell. 'I really hope you can forgive me.'

He doesn't move – just his hand, going up to his face then dropping back down again. Just his lungs, exhaling smoke towards Benjamin's ceiling.

'I don't want you back in my life,' he says to me. He rolls over and stares at me. 'You understand? I don't want you in my life.'

I nod but I don't really understand. I'm just hoping this is what it will take for him to get up and leave and not call the police.

'I don't want you to come to my apartment. And I really, really, really do not want you to tell your father any of this.'

'Derek?'

'Yes, sorry,' he says. 'Not your father. Derek. I don't want Derek to come around here asking questions. I'm perfectly happy the way I am.'

I sit back down on the couch. 'I'm sorry,' I say again. 'I don't really understand what you're saying.'

'I thought I'd hidden myself pretty well.' He sits up, squeezes the tip of his cigarette between index finger and thumb until it stops smoking, and drops it in the pocket of his powder-blue vest. 'What gave me away?' He notices his wig has fallen on the floor and bends down to retrieve it. It sits lifeless in his lap. I feel like things are rapidly going downhill. I don't know how to answer.

'How did you know I was your mother?' he elaborates.

How did I know–

I stare at him, hard this time, unashamed. He's small. His hair is short, grotty, looks like he cut it himself with a pair of nail scissors; it's unpleasantly flat from being under his wig. He's light, bird-boned, fragile, snappable. He has wrinkles all around his mouth and the skin on his lips is peeling and dry. He looks like a woman and his eyes look like my eyes and his crooked teeth are crooked the same way mine are in the photos of my seven-year-old pre-braces self.

'You look like her,' I say. 'You look like me. And your arm is gone.' And I wonder really, how I did know. Because I did.

He – she – nods, squints at me, harder. 'You look more like her than like me,' she says.

'Her?' I ask.

'My lover. Your father-mother. Your other-mother. Her, you look like her.' She stands, tugs a wallet from out of her back pocket, opens it and pushes a picture in my face. 'You look like her.'

I take the wallet and try to see any resemblance between myself and the crushed magazine picture my mother has stuck behind finger-printed plastic. I guess our hair is similar. Not so much that anyone would comment on it. I pass the wallet back. 'I suppose so,' I say. 'Who is she?'

She tells me and I'm a little bit impressed; she isn't famous now but she was, once.

'She won't give you anything,' she says. 'Don't try.'

'You're not Amy anymore, are you?' I have to ask. We won't speak again, I can see that. This is my only chance.

'Somewhere in here I'm Amy,' she says, waving her hand around her heart. 'Sometimes I'm Amy, in my home, by myself. Mostly I am Andrei and that suits me well enough.'

I could ask, 'Why didn't you want me?' But I know it wasn't personal. I can see it wasn't about me, but about Amy. This person wasn't anyone's mother. And I remember, suddenly, that Derek had told me she did want me but that he had refused to let me go.

'I'm sorry we didn't know each other,' I say, and I am overwhelmed at that moment with just how sorry I am. I'd thought she was dead. I had been sad about having no mother but not about not having a specific mother. And here she is, my specific mother who I did not have. My eyes fill up and spill over.

He shrugs; she shrugs. 'If anyone is to blame, it isn't you. You least of all. You not at all. Have you been happy?'

I wonder if I have. If I hadn't, I think, I would surely have walked away from my life this week given how easy that would have been. I must have been happy, in some kind of stupidly reptile-like unrealised way. I nod. 'Sure,' I say.

'Good,' she says, and stands to go. I can't think of a thing to say that would stop her. If I thought she could fix things for me perhaps I would try harder.

'Paul,' she says, 'there is something you could help me with – if you wouldn't mind.' I feel an eagerness to please that's entirely unfamiliar to me so I stand up from the couch as though it will be something as simple as opening a jar with a sticky lid.

'I have a jar I can't open,' she says.

And so I follow her downstairs to her apartment.

The jar is much bigger than I had expected and I struggle a little to open it. When the lid finally gives, it releases a reek of throat-tearing chemicals and sludged-down human flesh.

'The lid's off,' I say unnecessarily.

'Thank you,' she says, 'can you please put it back on?' She's opening all the windows and turning on the extractor fan.

I ask, 'Is it your arm?'

She shakes her head. 'Derek left it here,' she tells me and I have no idea how that could be true but I might as well hear her out to the end. 'I think it belongs to your friend.'

'My friend?'

'Upstairs. Your friend. Derek was in love with her once.'

I can only address this one improbable point at a time. 'This is Benjamin's arm? Why would Dad have Benjamin's arm?'

'Her name is Benjamin?'

I nod, hoping she'll answer the question.

'I don't really know,' she says. 'He left it here, one time, years and years ago. But I'm pretty sure it's hers. Could you please take it up to her? I don't want it here anymore. Tell her – ask her if she remembers the time with the soup. I saw it in her head; I think she saw it in mine. She has my arm. But I don't want it. Tell her that: I don't want it.'

'What do you mean Derek was in love with her?' I'm still several revelations behind.

She shrugs. 'Ask your father. You should go now, please.'

I'm not ready to never see my mother again so I ignore her and sit at her kitchen table staring at the jar.

'Do you want to hear about how I was declared dead?' I ask her. She doesn't answer. 'Because I don't have a father and because Derek wiped my birth from the hospital records to get back at you Identity has declared me dead. I don't exist. I have no house, no job, no bank account. Nothing. Nothing. Nowhere to go and no way to support myself when I get there.'

'You're no one?' she asks me.

'That's right.'

'What a magical state of affairs! I'm jealous,' she says.

'You can have it,' I say knowing that won't solve anything.

'Really? I would love to be no one. To owe nothing to anybody; just live without another person watching.'

I don't understand what she means. But she is holding her wallet again and she pulls out a laminated card and passes it across the table to me.

'Now give me yours,' she says.

It's an ID card – the card for Andrei Andropov. I flip it over and read the details: this address, a birth date 41 years in the past. She slaps a credit card down on top of it, 'This is yours too.'

'What are you doing?'

'Don't you want to be somebody?' she says.

'I want to be me!'

She shrugs. 'There's nothing I can do about that. But he could be you. You can become him. Everyone changes. You can't stay you your whole life.' She pushes the ID and credit card towards me again. 'He's OK, he's not bad. No dirty secrets. Do you think I'm trying to frame you for an unsolved murder?' She grins at me wickedly.

I sigh, take my own ID card from my wallet and give it to her. 'It doesn't work,' I say. 'That guy is dead.'

'Perfect,' she says. 'Rent is due the last day of the month. On Tuesday night and Thursday night at 7, go to the Community College. You teach Russian Literature. You should wear this.' She passes me the wig. 'And you'll need this.' She pulls a copy of *The*

Idiot from the bookshelf and hands it to me. I flick through the pages.

'Is this blood?' I ask her but she isn't listening.

'You get paid every second Wednesday but there's already a few thousand dollars in there,' she taps the credit card.

'Rent?'

'On this place. It's Andrei's so I guess it's yours now.'

'No, no; no that's no good.' For so many reasons. I can't live downstairs from Benjamin, for starters. Not now, not yet. And of course I can't throw my mother out on the street.

'It's yours,' she says. 'Don't worry,' she places the palm of her hand on top of my head and smiles at me, 'I have places to go.' She turns away from me, takes a key from a hook by the stove, and places it on the table in front of me. 'Here. I'll be gone the day after tomorrow, and it's yours. If you are here,' she smiles again, 'I will know where to find you.'

'I won't know where to find you.'

'True. Nothing will have changed. OK, now shoo, I have things to pack. Take the jar; don't go without taking the jar.' She picks up the rubbish bin, takes it into the bathroom and locks the door behind her. I can hear the sound of bottles being sorted and chucked.

How could Dad be in love with Benjamin? Shouldn't one of them have told me? If I knew what a tether was I'm pretty sure I'd know I was at the end of it. I pull an old envelope from my mother's paper recycling and write a note, pick up the key, the cards and the jar and leave.

2022: BENJAMIN

'Hello, this is Derek Crawford speaking.'

She nearly hung up the phone.

'Hello?' he said. She didn't recognise his voice. She'd expected she would. 'Is anyone there?'

'Derek. Hi.' She cleared her throat. Would he have recognised her? Don't be stupid. 'Derek, this is– this is Benjamin. I had a message to–'

'Benjamin? Benjamin! I was – how are you? *Where* are you?'

'I'm here, at my place. Paul said you wanted me to call.'

'Paul? You know Paul?'

'I know Paul. But you know that, right?' She was confused. She picked up the note again. *Derek came by while you were at work. He dropped this off for you, asked if you could call him on 0631228476* 'He said I should call you about this jar.'

'Jar?'

'Jar.' She read the note out to him.

'What kind of jar is it?' he asked.

'You didn't leave me this jar, did you?' She wasn't asking. 'It's really big, medical looking, brown glass.'

'Oh. That jar. Where did Paul get hold of that jar?' He wasn't talking to her.

'Derek – did you leave a message for me to call you?'

'I didn't. But I'm so glad you did. Benjamin! Benjamin, how are you? Where are you? In the city?'

'Yeah, in the city. And you – well, you're Paul's dad, aren't you. You live down at the coast with your dog . . .' The pieces were falling into place as the words came out of her mouth and she almost burst out laughing. Had she really? It seemed she had. She didn't have time to think about it now.

'I am. I do. How do you know Paul?'

'Oh, friend of a friend or something. I didn't realise he was your son until, well, just now really.' She needed to get off the subject of Paul. 'So this jar is nothing to do with you?'

'I wish I could say that were true. I think that jar has your arm in it. But I have no idea where Paul got it.'

'My arm?'

'Your arm. You see, I was minding it for you and–'

'Hang on.' She cut him off, put the phone down and crouched on the floor by the front door so she could see into the jar. She tapped the glass and through the liquid murk saw a pale, bobbing limb. She picked up the phone. 'I think I'll have to call you back.'

'No wait, wait! Wait. Don't go.'

She sat and stared at the jar – she didn't feel safe turning her back on it.

'Where has it been all this time?' she asked him.

'I left it at Amy's,' he said.

'Amy's?'

'My wife. Ex-wife. Paul's mother. I left it with her. You see, I was minding it for you and–'

'What the fuck, Derek? Why did you give my arm to your wife?' Wasn't he supposed to be building a shrine to her?

'I don't know.'

'I have to go.'

'No, hang on! I took your arm after you left, after you checked out. I stole your arm. I was looking after it!' He paused, but she didn't reply so he pushed on. 'You're right. I was out of my mind, Benjamin. I was very upset. By all of it. I took your arm. And later, I don't know when, a year, two? Later. I had it with me when I went to see Amy, to talk about custody, about Paul. And I left it behind. And then I didn't want to go back for it.'

'I see. You stole my arm from the hospital '

'The case was finished. You still got your money, didn't you?' He sounded worried.

'I got my money, yes. You didn't ruin that. So you stole my arm and accidentally left it at your wife's house during a fight?'

'That's about it.'

'And now Paul has left it at my apartment with a note claiming it was dropped off by you.'

'If you say so.'

'I do. Hang on.' She put the phone down again and re-read the note.

Dear Benjamin, I have to go up north. A friend there says he might be able to sort out my ID but it will take a few months. He says I'll need to 'lie low'. I might not see you again. But thanks for everything, I really appreciate it.

Also, Derek came by while you were at work. He dropped this off for you, asked if you could call him on 0631228476.

She had no idea what any of that meant, except that Paul was apparently dumping her and that – wait a second – he was setting her up with his dad just like he'd kept threatening to do.

She picked up the phone again. 'Are you still there?'

'I'm still here.'

'I guess Paul found his mum.'

'I guess I'm going to be in for another telling off over dinner tonight then. Unless he's staying with that girl– he– met– oh.'

'Can we not?'

'Perhaps best.'

They were both silent for a while. Eventually Derek spoke.

'And is that it, then? Would you have called me if this hadn't happened?' he sounded a bit miffed.

'I don't know. It's complicated.'

'Clearly.'

'Derek, it was twenty years ago. You're married again?'

'I'm not married again. I didn't even get around to getting divorced. I wasn't very impressed you left without saying goodbye, you know. That was very hurtful.'

Hurtful? He sounded like it was still hurtful. Surely he hadn't been pining for her the whole time.

'You?' he said. 'You've married?'

'I'm not married,' she said. 'Never really saw the point.'

'No, me neither,' he said.

There was silence again, for a moment, then he said, 'Benjamin. I can't believe it's you. Do you want to, well, catch up?' he asked. 'Just a coffee or something.'

'I have to go, Derek. I'm sorry, I have to go.' The arm. He'd stolen her arm. She needed some time to think about all of this.

'Can I call you back? Later, perhaps. On this number? Please, don't just disappear again.'

She didn't know. She really just didn't know. 'Yes,' she said, 'of course. Of course. We should talk, say hello. That would be nice. Call me. Or I'll call you. Something. Soon, OK, sorry, I really have to go,' and she hung up the phone.

She put her forehead down on her arms and waited for the rain to start.

Oh, man. She leant forward on her knees, leant her head on her knees and stared at the carpet. Watched her tears hit the carpet, sit there, watched the surface tension break, saw them soak in.

She walked to the kitchen and poured herself a glass of orange juice. Drank the juice without tasting it. Stood at the kitchen counter and stared at the pulp left sitting in the bottom of the glass, waiting for something to happen, waiting to feel a little bit less like she'd been kicked in the stomach. Nothing happened. She bent over double and pressed her hands into her belly.

She couldn't decide what music to put on. She lay on her back on the floor. Twenty-two years. She should be old by now. They could have been old together, be living together in a house in the suburbs, worrying about their kids off at college drinking too much beer, failing class, getting girls pregnant. They could be worrying about sexual dysfunction. She'd never even had sex with him when he wasn't worrying about sexual dysfunction. They could have got a dog. He had a dog. He had all that stuff. What if he'd had all that stuff with her? She imagined herself in that life. She'd have been Paul's mum. Jesus.

She peeled herself off the floor and eyeballed the jar. She hefted it into the kitchen, up on to the sink and opened the lid; the smell was appalling. She gagged, thought about vomiting, then thought about vomiting into a bag and leaving it on her downstairs neighbour's doorstep, which made her laugh and made a little bit of spew come out her nose.

She sat on the kitchen floor for a minute until things were under control.

OK. She tipped the jar on its side and let the reeking formalin gurgle its sludgy brown way down the plughole. She couldn't get the last bit out without the arm slipping out with it and so there it was, all wrinkled and juicy, lolling in the bottom of the sink. She was never giving herself another pedicure in that sink – that was for sure.

'Hi arm.'

It didn't look familiar. She'd somehow thought it would, but it didn't.

'Sorry about all this.'

She stared.

'I don't think they can put you back on. Not now. I'm sorry. I didn't mean for it to end like this. I wish we could have stayed together. Ah, crap.'

No more crying. No more! She took a deep breath. Oh, Jesus, the smell!

'OK arm, here's the deal. I'm taking you down to the park and burying you, OK? OK. Good.'

So she pulled an ugly sarong out from the bottom of a pile of stuff she'd meant to dump at the thrift store, wrapped the arm up and put it in a shopping bag. She closed the door quietly behind her and snuck down the stairs. She headed for the hardware store to buy a spade.

—

The letter had shown up yesterday afternoon, two weeks after she'd buried her arm, the paper old and crushed. Crushed and smoothed, crushed again, resmoothed. It felt like soft cotton.

> *I miss you. If I had even the foggiest idea where you were, I'd come to your house right now and hug you and scratch behind your ears because I love you and I miss you.*
>
> *For a long time before you came along, my self had huddled inside its dark meaty cell. But you got past this wall of flesh and expectations to cradle my tired brain in your safe hands. When I gave you my darkest thoughts you took them to the park, played with them, tickled their tummies and sent them back to me with smiles on their faces. Your words wrapped a warm blanket around me and your skin smelt like home. I wanted to curl up and sleep forever in the nimbus where our edges smeared.*

It was dated November 26 2000. And at the bottom, in pencil, newer and fresher, a phone number and the letter D.

She looked at herself in the mirror, at the short-cropped hair streaked with grey, the delta of delicate crows' feet, the tiny broken vein by her nose. What had Paul told him about the two of them, about this 22-year-old chick he knew called Benjamin? Was that who he was writing to? She wasn't that 22-year-old anymore. It had all gone down the sink with the formalin.

She smoothed the paper between her fingers, thought of the curve of his jaw, his hand holding hers under the hospital sheet when he thought she was asleep. She thought of all the time that had passed. She thought about how he'd stolen her arm.

She lay on the floor. Her neighbour was back. For days she'd heard nothing from him but there he was again, muttering into his heating duct.

'Why is it that when you awake to the world of realities you nearly always feel, sometimes very vividly, that the vanished dream has carried with it some enigma which you have failed to solve? You smile at the extravagance of your dream, and yet you feel that this tissue of absurdity contained some real idea, something that belongs to your true life, something that exists, and has always existed, in your heart.'

She rolled over and yelled into the duct, 'Can you

please shut the fuck up down there!' but he kept right on reading.

EPILOGUE – 2023: PAUL

'So Andrei,' he says to me, 'great class. I never knew *The Idiot* could be so . . . so, *relevant*. How long you been teaching Russian literature?'

'Decades, my friend; is decades,' I tell him. 'Since arriving here from Russia, has been almost twenty years.'

'You carry it well, my friend. Very, very well. This table OK?' he says, grabbing a spot near the bar and with a view of televised football. I nod and we sit.

'So this'll sound weird but I never forget a face and I'm pretty sure I saw you one time out near the hospital. On the bus? Gotta be a year back now. Pretty sure it was you.' He leans back, puts his feet up on a chair and I cannot help but notice his footwear. *'Koroshaya obuv,'* he says, gesturing to his shoes. 'Am I right?'

I nod and smile.

While he watches the football I skim once more the letter from my mother, telling of her new life on a farm with a cat and an armchair, her questions about my course, of whether I would again teach *Letters from the Underground* or choose this year to focus on *The Brothers K.*

Perhaps I should introduce myself to the new upstairs tenant, I think. Now I am 42 I should be meeting older ladies. She seems very appropriate. Very attractive. A little familiar.

My beer is empty. My student's too. 'Let me get you another drink,' I tell him and stand up, adjusting my wig.

ACKNOWLEDGEMENTS

The first draft of this story was written at the turn of the century, when I lived in San Francisco. It owes its existence, ideas and characters to the City. Thank you to Brett Fechheimer, Peter Morris, Wendy Smith, Michele Posner and John Spelman for japes, whiskey, carpool, Sopranos, smut, songs, insights, food reviews and arguments. Thanks in particular to Laurel Savino, my first-ever writing partner, and to Robert Reid, the guy in #27, who loved those crazy Russians, who left notes about earplugs and who was always worth impressing.

Thank you to Marisa Wikramanayake, *Formaldehyde*'s editor, for being a damn sight better than I am at spotting the difference between present and past tense and for picking up some rather dangerous discrepancies. Editors are the best. And thanks also to Roses Mulready and Michael for the time they took to read drafts and give such helpful feedback.

And thank you always to Andy, for being patient and funny and understanding and for listening to me read the same manuscript out loud over and over and over.

Available online and from discerning book retailers

VIVA LA NOVELLA 2015 WINNERS

Welcome to Orphancorp by Marlee Jane Ward
978-1-921134-58-6 (print) | 978-1-921134-59-3 (digital)

Formaldehyde by Jane Rawson
978-1-921134-60-9 (print) | 978-1-921134-61-6 (digital)

The End of Seeing by Christy Collins
978-1-921134-62-3 (print) | 978-1-921134-63-0 (digital)

VIVA LA NOVELLA 2014 WINNERS

Sideshow by Nicole Smith
978-1-922057-97-6 (print) | 978-1-921134-24-1 (digital)

The Other Shore by Hoa Pham
978-1-922057-96-9 (print) | 978-1-921134-23-4 (digital)

The Neighbour by Julie Proudfoot
978-1-922057-98-3 (print) | 978-1-921134-25-8 (digital)

Blood and Bone by Daniel Davis Wood
978-1-922057-95-2 (print) | 978-1-921134-22-7 (digital)

VIVA LA NOVELLA 2013 WINNER

Midnight Blue and Endlessly Tall by Jane Jervis-Read
978 1 922057 44 0 (print) | 978 1 922057 43 3 (digital)